BURN

a novel

Stephanie Austin

BURN

a novel

Stephanie Austin

Cowboy Jamboree Press
good grit lit.

Cover Design: Adam Van Winkle
Cover Art: Alexander Stanton
Interior Design: Adam Van Winkle

Cowboy Jamboree Press
good grit lit.

www.cowboyjamboreemagazine.com

Praise for Stephanie Austin and *BURN*

"*BURN* is filled with beautiful losers covered in scars of their own making. And yet it also finds hope in the dark places, both real and in the mind. A stunning, assured, and risky debut."

–Tod Goldberg, *New York Times* bestselling author

"*BURN* is gritty, pretty and real, highly entertaining—like a 'beach read,' only if the beach were a good dive bar, *BURN* is a novel to sink into and enjoy every moment."

–Monica Drake, author of *Clown Girl*

"Clear your calendar: once you pick up *BURN*, you won't put it down until the final, aching word. In Shannon, Stephanie Austin has created an antiheroine for the ages, a young woman equally bent on self-destruction and surviving any way she can. I saw parts of myself in her I didn't want to see, and I couldn't look away."

–Jennifer Wortman, author of *This. This. This. Is. Love. Love. Love.*

"Stephanie Austin's *BURN* is a raw, unforgettable debut novel that ignites from the first page and never lets go. Step into Shannon's chaotic world—a gritty, heartbreaking journey that doubles as a love letter to the 90s. These characters will steal your heart, break it, and make you laugh through the tears. Austin's writing is fearless and devastatingly beautiful, cementing her place among today's most powerful voices. *BURN* doesn't just tell a story—it consumes you, leaving you scorched and begging for more. This is a debut ready to set the literary world ablaze."

–Danny Goodman, author of *Amerikaland*

"In *BURN*, Austin jolts the reader into the mind of Shannon, a lonely young woman whose every attempt at connection leaves her more isolated than before. Set in the grimy and hypnotic world of 90's college-age partying, *BURN* asks how anyone raised amid sexualized violence can ever escape its patterns, even when they recognize them. A heartbreaking novel, *BURN* will leave a reader singed but ultimately hopeful for women who must navigate the world with a smashed compass."

–Amanda Bales author of *Pekolah Stories*

"Stephanie Austin's *BURN* is a gripping and unforgettable journey of transformation. Austin weaves a powerful tale of passion and survival, as flames of change threaten to consume everything. One woman is pushed to the brink as relationships ignite and collapse, as her courage is tested and she must reshape her one destiny. With vivid storytelling and emotional intensity, *BURN* delves into the heart of what it means to endure and rise from the ashes."

–Brittany Ackerman, author of *The Brittanys*

For C.R.J.

Do you have any items of emotional significance to your life that you would be willing to sell? You determine the price based on its value to your past.

Now is the time to take stock of your history and your things. Start clean.

—flyer in a coffee shop in Tempe, AZ in 2005, name unknown

PART ONE:

The Hotshot

1999

CHAPTER 1

The inside of the Love's off the I-40 feels like most places you'd end up in when you're avoiding everything: hot, fluorescent, overwhelming, and sad. A group of guys blow in behind me dripping in Benton's colors. They are faded and off-putting, like old cologne and an after-hours party. Laughing, they make for the hot dogs. I am also hungry. Not hungry. And wildly mesmerized by the hot dogs. They go around and around wasting their lives. That yellow lamp makes them look sick and burned, and they don't even care.

But Christ, it's hot in here. I peel off my down jacket, roll up the sleeves on my flannel but stop short of taking it off because my shirt underneath is a whole thing: see-through and provocative on purpose. My mouth is dry and cottony, and when I swallow, I taste old cigarettes. An hour's drive left. The sun is pretty much gone. Arizona mountain weather in January? Bipolar. You never know if it's up or if it's down. Dress in layers, save yourself.

The guys swarm the hot dogs now, handle the buns first, then put the hot dogs between them. They add ketchup, mustard, and relish. One of them watches me watching him.

"You want?" he asks.

"I'm sorry, what?" I ask.

"You look like you want a wiener," he says, and they laugh and laugh and laugh and laugh.

I had a wiener last night. So no. No wieners for me.

"I'm fine," I say, itchy now for a cigarette.

"Are you sure? Here, you can have this one. I can make a new one. I can make as many as you want," he says, wiggling it at me.

My stomach, warm and sour, feels like it's outside pressing in. I didn't take a shower before I crawled out of Andy's house this morning. I like to keep his smell on me, in me. The other friend they came in with has a case of beer over his shoulder, like he's some kind of lumberjack, and is calling for them to hurry the fuck up. These assholes are definitely on their way to Benton.

I need caffeine. A kick up. Shaking and sweating and with a renewed urgency to get out of here, I pour a big cup of coffee and dump sugar and powdered creamer in it, stirring for a long time. The creamer does not blend. I hold my hand over the cup and feel nothing because the coffee is broken, so I leave it and pull a Cherry Coke out of the fridge.

A shaggy-haired man comes in, cuts in front of me, goes straight to the counter and asks for a pack of cigarettes. I put my hands up. I don't want trouble from this guy. Go ahead. Do your business and get out of here. The cashier, gangly like a newborn deer and covered in big blotches of brown freckles, takes the guy's cash and gives him a handful of change. The man spends some time carefully putting the coins away in the various pockets in his Army jacket.

"Your M&M's in that soup don't float," the man says.

"Have a nice night, Sir," the cashier replies.

The shaggy-haired man stares at me but doesn't move. "M&Ms," he shouts.

Another man, older-looking guy. 40ish? Wearing a Packers beanie, black sweatshirt. He steps out of line to say to the M&M shouter: "Sir, you need to step outside."

The shaggy-haired man takes a step forward but stumbles. He's drunk or high or both. He loses his balance, grabs onto the counter. The man in the Packers beanie walks to the door and opens it. The shaggy-haired man shuffles away, still mumble-shouting about the M&Ms.

"Next," the cashier says.

I step forward. "You've got a coffee situation over there."

"The burners go in and out," the cashier says.

Another trucker opens the door letting in a blast of cold air. That's what this place is. Truckers and college kids. From the outside: "M&Ms!" The trucker kind of stops, looks at the shouter but then comes all the way in, disappears into the massive stretch of bullshit called the inside of a truck stop: batteries, granola bars, meat sticks, magnets, and car fresheners. At the counter at the diner attached to the truck stop, two men in flannels stare up at the TV news. A picture of Monica Lewinksy shows up on the screen. One man says something to the other. They laugh. Next, Clinton. They don't have much to say about him.

The cashier rings up my Cherry Coke. Next to a rack of Slim Jims is a little basket of sad-looking chocolates. The sign reads .65 a piece. Someone wrote the name "Carla" then drew an arrow to the .65. Carla is probably worth more, and I almost say that, I almost go all the way there with this guy, but then I keep my mouth shut. He doesn't give a shit who wrote it. Maybe he wrote it. The cigarettes behind him sparkle. I haven't had a cigarette since last night. Or, this morning, I guess. Whatever time we all passed out. I threw up so fucking hard this morning, I have broken blood vessels around my eyes. All that poison trying to get out. This time? Quitting for real.

I pay for my drink and escape, congratulating myself. Temptation didn't win. Delay gratification. See how that feels. Outside, I unroll my sleeves, put my jacket back on and open my car, plunk into the driver's seat, put the keys in. I flip my vanity mirror down and turn on the dome light. It feels fucking bad is how it feels. My mascara is smudged, so I use my middle fingers to wipe it away. Guy outside my car lights up. Fresh cigarette smell: a hard mistress.

I turn my key to start the car, but it doesn't start. The lights come on. So does Fleetwood Mac. The engine clicks. Doesn't turn over.

I take the keys out. Car goes dark. I put them in again, turn. Nothing. Click, click, click.

I turn the key one more time. The endless clicking of clicks. It's dead. The car is fucking dead.

I get out of the car. Slam the door. I stomp over to the pay phone, open the side pocket in my purse where I keep my quarters.

I drop the quarter in and dial my apartment hoping Rebecca will answer. The line rings and rings and rings, and I'm about to hang up when the machine picks up, damn it. Blah-blah-blah, this is Rebecca and Shannon, leave a message.

"Rebecca? Are you there? Rebecca? Can you hear me? My car is broken down. Rebecca? I need some help. I'm at the Love's. I need a ride. Hello? Rebecca?"

The quarter gets swallowed up.

A whisper in my brain: *call Andy.*

I hold the quarter up, ready to drop it. The whisper gets louder. Andy. Andy. Andy. *Call him.* Call him.

I insert the quarter and as I dial, the flood of anxiety and joy surge though I never know how he'll react to me.

A female voice says hello. Cassie, his roommate's girlfriend. She covers the receiver with her hand, and I hear her call out for *Andy! Phone!* A pause. *I don't know.* Huffy, she comes back on the line. "Who is this?"

I tell her it's me, Shannon. She knows me. Cassie and me, we're sort of friends. We hung out last night. The two of us in the backseat. Brian, her boyfriend, driving. Andy in the passenger seat with a pipe that looks like a cigarette. They can't tell, Andy said. It looks like a cigarette? See? Yes, because people inhale cigarettes long and deep. Because cigarette smoke smells like marijuana. Brian blasting Alice in Chains so loud it dove into my body, ripped it apart from the inside out. Cassie slapping herself in the face because she was numb from the coke. All of us getting jostled by Brian's drunk driving. All of them a little pissed at me because I'm only 20, still can't get into the bars, so we had to go to The Island, which is where the high school kids go to party.

Silence. She covers the receiver again. Muffled voices. A trucker strolls by. Stops.

"Hey," he says.

15

I angle away.

"Hey," he says again.

I glance over at him.

"Smile. It's not that bad."

So I do. I smile. It's easier. Now I can have my conversation.

Andy comes on in a thick voice, "Hello."

"Hey! Long time no talk!"

"What?" He sounds confused, like he was asleep but it's late in the afternoon. Like, I am still unbelievably hungover, but I've been somewhat with it the last few hours.

"I mean, I saw you this morning. Calling again so soon? Yes, I am."

On the other end of the phone, I hear gurgling and a deep intake of breath.

"Anyway, so I am halfway to Benton. Remember? I was going back to school. So, yeah, my car is stalled. I'm at the Love's. That big truck stop."

An exhale, then a lot of coughing.

"Hello?" I ask.

"Yeah?"

"So my car won't start."

"That sucks."

"It does. It does suck. What could it be? The car clicks. But won't start."

"I don't know."

"Yeah, so I called because I thought, well, Andy is a mechanic. He knows about cars because that's his job, right? Hahaha."

"Maybe a dead battery."

I look down, realize I've wrapped the cord around my wrist, so tight it's cutting off my circulation. Dead battery. Dead, dead battery. Battery. Dead.

"Maybe you could drive up here and, um, jump me. Then maybe come up to Benton for a few days. It's really cold here, but it's a real season. Nice change from the valley, right?"

We can drink cocoa and eat marshmallows. Get cozy with each other under a blanket.

"Someone around there can probably give you a jump," he says.

I won't cry here. I've learned not to push him. Not ask too much at one time. I've broken my own rule. My own fault. I wanted more time with him, and over break, he seemed, for the first time in a long time, interested in giving it to me. But now? He feels distant again.

"All right, wanted to check in with you. Yes. So I have to go figure out how to get out of here," I say as cheerful as possible.

"I meant to tell you," he goes on and it stops me. "I'll be in Benton soon."

"For my birthday?" I am momentarily elated.

"My buddy is getting married," he says.

"Oh. Yes!" Whatever pit I'd started to swerve into, I pull up.

"Yeah, I'll call you," he says. Another gurgle, another deep, sucking breath.

Andy is high all the time, all the time he is high. He is high before work. He is high after work. His favorite thing? Get high and sit in the shower. He'll smoke a huge bowl and then turn the water on and sit in the tub while the shower pours over him. You are participating in rebirth. I said that once. He blinked. Had no idea what I was talking about. Andy's got a lot of shit going on. Dead dad. Died a few years ago. Heart attack at work. I was like, dude, I fucking wish my stepdad was dead. Do you know how much better my life would be if that motherfucker dropped dead? Andy's pot thing doesn't bother me. Whatever you need to get by is what you need to get by. Don't get caught, right?

Andy is coming to Benton, and his friend is getting married, and he wants me to go with him, and he wants me to meet a wider swath of his friends, and this time—this time—he will want me longer. He will want to stay.

The Packers beanie man is inside, still. I eye him at the cash register. Earlier, he felt helpful.

One quarter left. I insert it. Dial my mother. A gamble. She won't recognize the number. She may not answer.

"Baker residence," she says, almost too happily.

"It's me," I say, relieved to hear her voice.

"Hi Shannon, how are you?" she asks.

Her voice is strained and overly pleasant.

"Oh," I say. "He's home."

"Yes," she says. "That's so good to hear, honey."

"I thought he'd be at work by now," I say.

"Boy do I know that," she says. "Plans change."

My stepfather doesn't like her talking on the phone, so we have a code for if he's home or not home, which translates to how freely she can speak. He thinks it's all a secret plot. My car is stuffed to the gills with black garbage bags. Her clothes. Shoes. Things she'll need when she comes up for my birthday and then never go back. So, I mean, I guess this time it is a secret plot but usually it's just me needing to hear her voice so I know she's okay.

"Mom, I—"

"That's really great, honey," she cuts me off. "Hold on one second."

She puts the phone on her shoulder, maybe, or cradles it in her neck. She calls the dog. She's stepping outside, pretending like she's letting the dog out. I hear wind now, brilliant and alive. The difference between in the house and out of the house is unreal. They live in the desert, near a wash, so the wind is always gusting.

"Are you ok?" she asks.

I hear concern in her voice, and it allows me to relax, almost give in, let her know I am not, and never have been, okay, but then, behind her, I hear my stepfather's voice, pushing, angry. He's yelling something about coffee. Making it. Buying it. They're out. He needs her more than I do is what he's saying, has always said.

I sigh. "You better go take care of him, Mom." I don't mean to be shitty and entitled, but she takes it that way. Feels the need to defend herself.

She lowers her voice, slightly. "Honey, please. Please, please, please—yes, all right dear, one second ok?"

The pain in her voice is like glass under my skin.

Then she perks up, because he must have followed her outside and says, "That's really good to hear, honey." The phone is muffled. "It's Shannon. Just saying she's made it back to school."

The man with the Packers beanie is walking toward the exit. Another trucker walks past me, and I shrink into the phone booth.

"Happy start of spring semester!" she prattles on. "And listen, be careful. All right? You be careful. Don't walk at night. Be aware of your surroundings. Remember to hold your keys between your fingers like I showed you."

"All right, see you later," I say and hang up.

The horror of my tone sets in as I imagine her standing outside, pretending to say goodbye to me. My stepfather accuses me of not loving my mother enough. Once again, I take in all the bags in my car. She'll be free soon enough. We have to do this a little longer. It's fine. It's all going to be fine.

Here comes the Packers beanie guy. I hurry into my car, open the door and try to start it again. Click, click, click, click, and more clicks. He steps outside. Appears to be on track to walk past me, so I pop the hood, and he stops.

"Everything all right?" he asks.

"Dead battery," I say.

He comes closer. "Do you mind?"

I let this stranger sit in the driver's seat. He turns the key. Click, click, click, click.

"If it's clicking, it isn't the battery," he says.

My stomach drops. He glances into the back seat filled with my mother's black trash bags.

"You moving bodies?" he asks.

I'm saving my mother.

"On my way back to school," I say. "Could it be the fuel pump? I had to replace that a few months ago. Maybe it was a busted one."

This car has ruined me. That fuel pump costs me hundreds of dollars I don't have. Now this? He gets out of the car and peers into the hood. Our chatter has drawn the attention of another man. This one in a heavy flannel, khakis and a red hat. He has a flashlight. The two of them reach under my hood, press on things, turn things, do whatever secret things grown men do inside car engines.

"Could be the starter," the man in red says. "Can you get a ride? Benton's not far. You'll have to get it towed is my guess."

The man in the Packers beanie, when I don't answer, perhaps senses from the frozen look on my face that I am unprepared and helpless, picks my purse up off the ground, nods toward the car.

"Lock her up," he says. "Grab your things. You don't want to hang out here by yourself. I'm going through Benton. I can give you a ride."

The other man, hands in his pockets, walks off. The hot dog assholes are gone. I'm trapped. I'm cold. I want to go home. I turn the key again, the car lights up and I extract *The Dance*, which I often listen to on repeat, especially after seeing Andy. I stick the disc in an empty sleeve in my CD case, notice the second empty sleeve and realize I left Fiona Apple in Andy's room. "Left." He went through my CDs, took it out, played it, then didn't put it back. Perhaps it was intentional. Perhaps he wanted to hang onto something that reminded him of me. I stuff the garbage bags into the trunk, which is bursting. The man in the Packer's beanie still holds my purse.

"Hold on," I say and pop back into the store.

I walk up to the counter. The guy behind it was staring out into the nothing.

"Hey, I'm leaving my car here," I say and thumb out the door.

"Ok," he says.

"Don't let anyone steal it," I say.

"Sure," he says.

The man leads me to his truck, helps me get up into it. I gather my things on me like a security blanket. He puts his seatbelt on, reaches into his visor for a pack of cigarettes. Camel Lights.

He holds the pack out to me. I take one. It will settle my agitation. He chatters on about his life trying, in my estimation, to put me at ease. He has a bunch of animals. Dogs, cats, horses, chickens, ducks. His wife raises them, sells them. Has some land. Land that's been in his family for generations. I crack the window so the smoke can escape. He asks me if I have towing insurance. No? He asks if I have a job. Sort of? He asks what I'm studying. Advertising. What am I going to do with that degree? A degree is a thing to have, not use. I'm about to flick my cigarette out the window. I roll it down a little further and this guy—Jim? I think he said his name was Jim—yells for me to stop. Like, he yells at me. Like, his anger is a stepfather level of anger.

"Hey," he says. "That's how brush fires start. Especially with this freak dry winter this season."

I close the window. Hold my bags closer to my body. The inside of the truck feels thick now, almost humid.

"I'm with Billy Joel," I say and put the cigarette out in the little can he has positioned in his console.

Feels like it takes him a second, but he gets it. Smirks a little. Starts chattering again. This time about the road. The road is long. The road can be draining. Long stretches of time without talking to other people. I stare out at the trees going by at 80 mph. Watch the little cars shoot past us. Even in winter, the pine trees stay green. I chose Benton two and a half years ago because of the trees. The seasons. The valley is great and all, but it's long stretches of brown dotted with cactus and

21

scorpions and black widows and lizards that sneak into your house.

He passes the first exit for Benton, which he doesn't take. And that's fine. It's too early. I told him I live on the east side, and there's plenty other exits. Like, that's the exit I take only because I don't like being on the highway but it's certainly not the only option.

We pass the second exit into Benton, which is, again, fine because there's bunches of other exits and he knows what he's doing. Trust. Ask for another cigarette. That's harmless. Demonstrate I am not afraid. Sir May I Have Another but here we are coming up on the third exit into Benton, and still, he does not slow down.

CHAPTER 2

I swallow, lick my lips. Attempt to generate moisture. I clear
my throat with a cough. Outside, I try to calculate how far
below me. What might happen to my body if I open the door
and jump. Who will be sad if I'm gone? My mother, of course.
My stepfather? Andy?

We come up on a battered Hadley's sign that's visible
from the freeway. I raise my hand. Point to it. Manage to choke
out, "There. My friend is waiting for me."

"Old Hadley's?" he asks but still doesn't slow.

Hadley's is the oldest diner in Benton.

"Yep, he's waiting," I say.

"Your boyfriend?"

I calculate the best answer. Will it stop him from
killing me if he knows I have a boyfriend?

"Yes," I say.

"I thought you said you lived in East Benton?"

"Uh, did I? This is better, actually. He's waiting for me.
I called him and told him I was coming."

He says nothing further, and as I'm about to open the
door and throw myself out of the truck, thinking a broken leg
or broken ribs is better than complete death, he eases his foot
off the gas and signals he's getting off the highway. He can't
pull all the way into Hadley's tiny parking lot, so he stops in
the quiet street.

I gather my things. "Thank you for the ride."

The truck is so high off the ground, I have to slither
down while holding my things.

"Get your car handled, and don't let them give you
any shit," he says over the console. Now that I am still alive,
and if I pretend, he sounds like a father. A man who cares
about your well-being. A man who does not want to see harm
come to you. A confusing man with two different vibes, but
that is, I suppose, not new.

Slamming the door shut is like moving a steel barrier.

Hadley's is an old brick standalone building. The parking lot is in shambles, white lines all gone, full of cracks. There are two trees, bare at the moment. Winter and all. The big open sign is lit up but the P is out. An old poster taped to the inside of the front window advertises French dips for $2.99. The truck pulls away, offers a honk.

Inside, it is empty save for one guy in a gray hoodie hunched over the counter, and then Daniel. He is disheveled, as usual. His khaki pants are wrinkled, and his hair is in a short ponytail with stray pieces he's now tucking behind his ears. He studies me, takes me all the way in, because me showing up at his restaurant is a trick he can't wait to take apart.

"Well, well," he says and crosses his arms. "Look what the cat dragged in."

"Hello, Daniel," I respond.

The person in the hoodie swivels around, walks a marionette out to me and holds her hand up in greeting.

"Hi, Adrian," I say. "Hello, Violet."

Daniel walks to the window. "Did you just get out of that truck?"

"Long story," I say. I sit, leaving a space between me and Adrian.

Daniel turns a mug over for me. He reaches into his back pocket for his flask. It is silver with an etching of deer antlers on the front. He pours a shot of what smells like whiskey into my cup. He takes a pull from the flask before he tucks it away again.

"Hair of the dog" is all he says. "Coffee will be a minute." He opens the coffee machine, dumps the old grounds into the trash, opens a new bag, punches a few buttons. The machine shudders and pops before it brews.

I shoot the whiskey. Gag a little. Nod for him to pour another.

The Sun Also Rises, Daniel's sacred and tattered text, sits open but face down on the counter. He picks up the book, closes it, puts it in his backpack. His notebook is open. His handwriting, long and cursive without space breaks, fills the pages.

Daniel wants to go to Paris to write the great American novel. He's been saving his money since as long as I've known him. He has a plan. Rent an apartment. Fill a hundred notebooks with metaphors about the human condition. The coffee machine spits and shudders. What Daniel wants, I believe this, is to live inside Hemingway's stories. He wants to take a train to Spain, sit in the stands of a bullfight. And it's like, Daniel, do you think you can handle that level of torture and death? Can anyone stomach that sort of thing?

Adrian maneuvers his puppet. When he catches me looking at him, he smiles. I think the same thing I always think when Adrian smiles. His mother is beautiful. The familiar smells of Hadley's—the French fries, the greasy hamburgers, the musty carpet, the commercial disinfectant—soothe me.

"You smell like old beer," Daniel says to me at the same time a pulsing beep comes out of Adrian's pocket.

Adrian lifts Violet. Her body lurches forward. Her glossy, black hair obscures her face, which he tucks behind her. He reaches into his pocket and pulls out a pager, clicks something on the side and looks at the number. Adrian reaches down next to him and plops a suitcase on the counter. Another puppet is in the case. The boy. Adrian puts the pager back in his pocket, removes his wallet, and pulls a twenty-dollar bill from a larger wad of cash inside his wallet. *Jesus Christ.*

"Since when do you have a pager?" I ask Adrian.

"Since awhile."

"I don't have your number. What if I need you for something?"

"What would you need from Adrian that you'd get through paging him?"

"I have no idea, but I don't want to be left out."

Adrian scribbles the number on a napkin, hands it to me.

"Where you headed?" Daniel asks.

"I gotta get these kids to bed." He zips his bag up.

"Is that it?" Daniel asks and takes Adrian's mug off the counter and brings it into the kitchen.

"Adrienne's coming over," Adrian replies. He puts his coat on.

I mouth *Adrienne?* to Daniel. He shrugs, rolls his eyes.

"I think we got some nice work done," Daniel says.

They guy hug. A handshake, backslap performance that wants to be a hug but can't get there.

"Thanks for the coffee," Adrian says and puts the twenty on the counter.

"You don't owe me anything," Daniel says.

"Take it," Adrian says.

But Daniel leaves it on the counter.

"Man, I'll miss this place," Adrian says.

"Be safe," Daniel says.

"That's a huge tip," I say.

Adrian picks up his suitcases, salutes both of us, and backs out the door as a car pulls into the parking lot and he gets into it.

"And there he goes, gentle into that good night," Daniel says. "Adrian is selling drugs."

"How do you know that?"

He gives me a dubious look. "I'm glad you're back."

"Are you?" I ask.

"I am," he says.

So much to process. Adrian is back. *Adrienne* is back. "What was he talking about? He'll miss this place?"

Daniel wipes Adrian's space with a gray rag that used to be white. "Boss Guy came in on Monday. He's closing. He sold the lot. They're going to tear the restaurant down."

"What?" I say. I am lightheaded now. "Why?"

Daniel waves his arms around. Empty booths. Empty chairs.

"When?" I ask.

"He says before summer," Daniel says. "I guess it works out anyway because—"

He stops himself.

"Because why?"

Daniel shakes his head. He arranges the salt and pepper shakers on the counter the way he was doing the first time I met him freshman year. Campus isn't far, and I walked over for coffee one morning because my Com class got out early and the coffee shack on north campus had a long line. I hadn't explored the town much, so it seemed like a good thing to do. We hit it off right away. And, like, it was no bullshit. We were friends immediately. We were friends like we'd known each other our entire lives.

The coffee machine beeps. He flings the towel over his shoulder and then pours me a cup. Even after adding cream and sugar, I still taste the whiskey. He's right though. The heaviness has lifted. I need both the up and the down, so I nod to his pocket. I'll take another shot.

"You look like someone died," he says.

"My car died."

"Oh shit. Where?"

"At the Love's."

"Shit," he says again.

I wave my hand. "I'll handle it. It's handled. Don't worry. I'll call a tow truck company."

"Sorry," he says. "That must have been scary."

I sip my coffee. I do not answer him.

"Pie?" He doesn't wait for me to answer, just takes a plate of sliced pecan pie out of the clear glass case that sits near the end of the counter.

He places it, and a rolled napkin with silverware, in front of me. The pie looks pristine and well-managed. Carving it up with a fork feels like a betrayal.

27

"I'm not asking you what you want," he says. "I'm telling you what you need."

A tiny, nearly imperceptible movement between his eyebrows. Maybe I'm not completely sober, and I'm making this into more than it is, but he knows. He knows I saw Andy over break. He knows why I'm hungover. I'm hyper-aware of the way I unwrap the silverware, work off the tip of the pie, and put it in my mouth. The sweetness mixes with the whiskey and the coffee. I take another bite, then another.

"It's hard to close chapters, you know?" he says. "But it was bound to happen. I was going to leave anyway. Someday."

"I mean, maybe you weren't going to leave or maybe you were."

He laughs. "Sure, yes. There's always this thing where you leave or don't leave places."

"When did Adrian get back?" I ask, sipping the whiskey-coffee.

"A few days ago," he says.

"He seems good," I say.

"He's focused on the marionettes," he says. "That's what he needs. He got a show. Did you know about that?"

"How would I know about that?"

He shrugs. "You're right. You didn't return my calls over break."

I can't look at him. "Yeah, you know, well, Shit Town was around a lot. He doesn't like us using the phone."

Daniel nods. He doesn't believe me, but he pretends he does. "Stellar's Jay. First Friday. Two months from now."

"I didn't know he was painting again."

"Not painting. A puppet show. I'm writing the script."

The whiskey brings the world down, mutes all the colors. "I'm confused. This is for kids?"

He laughs. "In no way is what I'm writing for kids, and in no way should anything Adrian ever does be for kids."

Where Daniel wants to plunk on a fedora, moisten the tip of his pen with his tongue and scribble notes into his notebook, Adrian wants to live inside his own depression. Adrian used to paint self-portraits. He'd draw his own face. Always sad or angry or both. And he'd paint over his face reds and blacks, and when you stare at one of those older paintings long enough, it feels like you've been in a car accident. Daniel has one in his living room over the dining room table. When I'm at his house, I almost can't look at it. It makes me sad for him. Or sad for myself. It makes me feel broken. Somewhere in the last year or so, Adrian left realism and moved toward abstract. His face became cartoonish. Then he stopped drawing. Stopped painting. Went home to Denver for a week then came back with these puppets. They belonged to his grandfather who died.

"Why didn't you call me to pick you up?" Daniel asks.

"Uh. Well, this guy offered. He was there already. I didn't want to wait. He was nice," I say. "He wasn't a killer."

Daniel's cheeks are tinged red. He wants to say more. He wants to know which guy, but he knows better than to ask that question in general. The clock past him reminds me how long this day has been. Rebecca is home now. Or maybe at Gary's. The booths behind me seem nice, wide-open, full of comfortable, artificial stuffing.

"Let's be good to our posture," Daniel says and points to the empty booth behind us.

The table top is chipped, and the exposed parts are covered with blue pen. Someone idled here. Scribbled. Tried to make sense. Made nonsense. Now that I'm sitting, I feel like I won't be able to get up. My body is heavy, like my skin is taking on water and dragging me down.

A picture of young, bloat-free Elvis hangs nearby. Dented salt and pepper shakers are pushed up against the wall like they're being punished. I close my eyes, realize how good they feel when they're shut. I press my fingers in on them. My body starts to settle. I think about dancing, how much I like

29

dancing, not really dancing, just swaying, just moving enough to get away from myself. The coffee is bitter.

"Shannon?" Daniel asks. "You ok?"

Silence drags itself between us like a rain-soaked cat, and I feel responsible for it, like I should pick it up, nurse it back to health. Bottle feed it, if necessary. And this seems like an end point, like one of those conversations you're in and suddenly a clock chimes or someone else needs your attention, which is God's way of closing the scene. If you even believe in God.

Meeting his eyes, briefly, enough to remember how brown they are, I say, "Do you have cigarettes?"

"Yeah," he says.

"Let's go smoke."

Daniel leads me through the kitchen. He nods to the cook. A little dude named Bobby who's leaning against the fridge, bored. Bobby is married, and Bobby also—according to Bobby—has a girlfriend.

"You can take off, man," Daniel says.

Bobby doesn't have to be told twice. He removes his apron and tosses it into the office on his way out. Smells like a hundred cows dying in a hundred tire fires back here. Daniel opens the back door, lets me go first with his hand hovering around my low back. Must have dropped ten degrees since I walked in. We plop onto the gray couch. Someone dumped it here like four months ago, and now we use it as a hang out.

He passes me a cigarette and a pack of matches. I light mine then hand it back.

Daniel is tinged with yellow from the light. Beside us, or in front of us, somewhere in the vicinity like out in the parking lot of the strip mall next to Hadley's, we hear what sounds like a plastic tub being kicked. I jump.

"Hey, you sure you're ok?" he says and leans in. "Come here." He reaches out to hug me, strokes my hair for a minute, two minutes. I relax into his body. I put my forehead in his chest. He pulls me tighter. And for a half a second—a half a fucking second, I feel like the day is reversing itself, like being in Daniel's presence is healing me, and if I try hard enough, the night before I left for winter break goes away, and we're the same two people we were when I left for home. But we're not. I sit up, settle on the end of the couch with space between us.

"Thank you for being a good friend," I say to the loose threads on the couch.

He puts his hand to his heart. "She called me a good friend. She didn't return my calls all winter break, not even to say Happy New Year, but I'm a good friend."

"My stepdad," I say vaguely.

"I know," he says. "He didn't tell you I called?" He appears ready to flick his cigarette.

"It's dry out there," I say.

"You're right," he says and drops it but stands, smashes it with his boot.

He wordlessly hands me his flask. I take a long, burning pull. "But hey, I have real news. It happened."

"You quit Andy?"

I hand the flask back. I don't answer. He huffs.

"My mom is leaving Shit Town," I say.

"She's not."

"She is."

"No way."

"She is. We packed up a bunch of her stuff in my car. She's coming for my birthday, then she's not going back." I see the look on his face. He doesn't believe me. We've been on this road. "She's never done that. She's never actually packed up her stuff. This feels real."

"Well, holy fuck."

Currently, all her stuff is stuck in my car which is stuck at Love's, but I'll figure that out. I will. I'll absolutely figure it out, the whiskey inside says so. Daniel nods for me to come back inside. I follow him. He walks to the door, turns the lock.

He pulls the food temp sheet out from under the counter. I don't think it's supposed to be kept there but whatever.

Then, a knock on the front door. I'm standing behind the counter. Daniel takes my arm and pulls me down. We sit on the filthy floor.

"Geez, you really need to mop," I say.

Daniel puts his fingers over his lips. "Shhh."

"The open sign is on," a man says. "Hello?"

Two old petrified French fries rest near us.

"This is why you're getting shut down, Daniel," I say and point to the French fries.

He points to the broom. Oh, like I'm welcome to sweep if I'm so disgusted?

"Why won't you let them in?" I whisper.

"I want to go home," he whispers.

Outside, I hear a woman say they should go to another place. The man insists though, continues to knock on the door harder and harder, like the idea of Hadley's being closed is a personal affront. I hear the woman's voice, quieter and softer than the man's, tell him to stop.

"No means no," Daniel says in a strange, deep voice.

This gives me whiskey giggles. He then army crawls away from me, which makes me laugh harder. He peeks out from the counter, gives me a hand signal. They're gone. He picks up his backpack, shuts off all the lights, and leads me out the back way to his car, an old black Toyota full of papers and Hadley's to-go cups. He starts the car, turns the vents away from me. The Beatles blast out.

"Ob-la-di, ob-la-da," Daniel sings along, thumping the steering wheel to the beat.

I roll my eyes.

"Sorry it's not the Spice Girls," he says.

"I barely listen to the Spice Girls," I say. "Can you take me through Jack in the Box?"

"Of course," he says.

His kindness is nice, but nice doesn't stick around. Nice is a cycle, and it feels like it's flying right now. Flying to blue jay way.

"You really know how to treat the inside of your car," I say, pointing to the mugs.

The streets are empty. Feels like we're the only ones alive. Where's Jim the Trucker? Long fucking gone. Back to all his animals. We approach the railroad tracks as the arms lower down. Daniel stops, leans forward to try to spot the train. The red lights flash against his face.

"What are you up to tomorrow?" he asks as he leans back.

"I gotta deal with my car. Get ready for school. A million things."

"What classes do you have again?"

"Uh. That history class because of the psychology debacle."

"Right."

"Graphic design. That's required—"

"Who do you have for graphic design?"

Daniel originally majored in advertising like me but switched halfway through to English. He took a bunch of advertising classes though.

"Gus-Something?"

"Gustavo?"

"Maybe."

"He's tough."

"Great." I feel dejected all over again.

He reaches into his pocket, pulls out a slip of paper.

"Forget all that. Come to this with me," he says, nodding to the paper. "Then I'll drive you around for school supplies."

Emotional Garage Sale.
Aurora Dahl welcomes your items of emotional significance.
75 W. Pointe Rd.

*You determine the price based on its impact in your life. Items sold on
consignment. Start fresh.*
Breathe again.

I trace the letters with my fingers. It's handwritten.
Someone sat down, took out a piece of paper, took out a pen,
and spent the time to physically write this out.

There's the Jack in the Box on the corner next to my
apartment. Drive-through is fast and easy. Daniel buys my
Sourdough Jack, says I don't owe him anything.

The gate to my apartment complex is still broken, so
Daniel drives right in. I open my car door.

"Seriously, glad you're back," he says. He punches a
button on his stereo and it spits out the disc. He digs around
under his seat and extracts the double CD case. The Beatles
White Album. He places the CD in the case and gives it to me.
"Listen to this album in its entirety three times through. You
will be cured."

"Of what?"

"Whatever it is that's wrong."

"Thanks for the ride," I say.

"I'll pick you up in the morning," he says.

"It's practically morning," I say.

My apartment is dark except for Rebecca's room. Her
door is wide open. Music blasting. My bedroom door is wide
open, too. Shouldn't be. I closed it before I left. Rebecca was in
there, rummaging around.

I walk by her door, ready to say hello, thank for not
answering the phone, when I see Gary's white ass up in the air
with Rebecca underneath him, head hanging off the bed
moaning. I roll my eyes and pull their door shut. The
answering machine on the counter is blinking. First message is
Daniel. Two days ago. Asking if I was back. Asking me to call
him. Saying he hoped I had a nice winter break. Erase. Second
message is my own voice from a few hours ago. Past me
standing outside a phone booth next to a broken-down car. The

desperation in my voice is unbearable. I erase it. The second is my mother, the desperation in her voice even more unbearable, and she's not all the way through saying *he's gone to work now, I can talk* when I erase her message, too.

I feel a little spinny and out of it, and the Jack in the Box didn't help. I undress and turn on the shower.

CHAPTER 3

So, it snowed. Just a little. Enough to blanket the trees. I open my bedroom door to light. Rebecca's opened all the blinds in our living room. The room spins. I have a vague sensation of falling, but then I shake it off. I should eat.

Rebecca sits on the couch watching *E!* She pulls her brown hair back in a messy bun, then tucks her bra strap under her black tank top. An empty, stained mug rests on the coffee table. She picks up the remote, clicks off the TV, stands and reties her pajama bottoms as she follows me into the kitchen.

"Your hair is curly," she says, accusatory.

"I went to bed with it wet," I say, pouring coffee into a chipped white mug.

She gasps. "You had to take a rape shower!"

"It was not a rape shower. I wanted to sober up before bed," I say, scanning the counter for sugar. "By the way, hello. Nice to see you."

"I hope you weren't driving drunk." She opens the cupboard, takes a new cup out, and pours fresh coffee.

A magnet on our fridge is a lobster wearing a bib with a lobster on it. It's holding a fork and a knife in its claws. We bought it on a spring break trip to Mexico last year. We thought it was funny the lobster was preparing to eat lobster.

I go to tell her I wasn't driving drunk—Daniel drove me, and he might have been drunk—but the creamer falls out of the fridge. Whoever put it in last—Rebecca—didn't close the lid very tight, so the creamer spills. Rebecca shoves wet paper towels in my hand, and we both bend down to wipe it up. Her nails are dark purple. She hums as she wipes up the mess.

Rebecca's fat-free raspberry coffee cake sits open on top of the microwave. I cut a slice with the knife that's stuck to the bottom of the box and set the piece in a napkin. I use what's left of the creamer and throw the empty in the trash, which is too full. A single plate is in the sink. I don't know what she did for dinner last night, but it involved cheese.

Out of habit, I go to my purse for my cigarettes, but instead I find my birth control pills. Shit. I open the pack. I've missed a few.

"It's ok," Rebecca says. She takes the blister pack from me. "What have you missed?"

"Two in a row, I think? What are you supposed to do? I don't remember? Skip them? Take them when you remember?"

"Have you had sex recently?"

I nod.

"With who?" she says, like it's a salacious detail. She hands me the pack back. "That Andy loser?" She shakes her head. "That guy sucks. You need to get over him. Anyway, just take them all now. If you're pregnant, the hormone surge will make you have a miscarriage. It's fine."

I swallow the two pills I missed and set a mental reminder to take the other one tonight at my usual time.

Rebecca perches over me. I open the phone book, turn to the yellow pages. T for Towing.

"Wait. Is your mom here?" she asks and looks into my room.

"No," I say. "That's next weekend."

ABC Towing. All Hands Towing. Butch's Towing. Does it matter?

"Gary and I are going out for breakfast. You want to come?" she asks.

Gary moved in across from us in September. He and Rebecca have been fucking ever since. He's 35. He's nice, I guess. He's unavoidable, really. He lifts weights with his curtains open.

"No thanks," I say. "Daniel is coming over in a bit."

"Oh, Daniel is coming over," she squeals.

"Why do you say it like that?"

"You've been gone forever, and the first person you see is Daniel? Ugh. Shannon. You have to just fuck him and get it over with. You're torturing him," she says.

"You think Daniel should be fucked, you fuck him," I say.

"Daniel is not my type," she says, tucking a piece of hair back into her bun.

"See? You don't even think he's hot," I say. "Andy is hot."

She rolls her eyes. "All right. Andy is hot. Andy is very fucking hot. I will give that to you. Good job on that front. Here's what I'll say. Daniel needs work. A haircut. New clothes. He could lose, like, 20 lbs. But then? Maybe."

"Well, he's not my type either," I say. "And he's my friend. It's not even like that." I stop. Did I tell her what happened before break? I don't think I did. I take the phone book and the phone into my room, but Rebecca follows. "Thank you. Have a nice brunch with your old man." I close the door in her face.

I call the first place. ABC Towing. No one answers. I call the second. All Hands. A gruff man says hello.

"Is this a towing company?" I ask.

"Yeah?"

"So. Hi. Yes. My car is broken down at the—um, at the Love's. You know where that is?"

"Yeah."

"Right. I need a tow back into Benton."

"Hold on," he says. I reach over to my nightstand and run my finger across. Dusty. I wipe it on my comforter. Which also smells dusty. After a minute, he returns to the phone. "What kind of car?"

"It's a Nissan."

"Nissan what?"

"Sentra. It's blue."

The man chuckles. "What year?"

"'88. I think."

"What's wrong with it?"

"I don't know. It wouldn't start." I hold myself up a little. "It's not the battery because the power comes on, and it clicks."

He makes a noise again. "All right. I can get out there Tuesday morning. Where you want it towed to?"

"Tuesday morning?" This is disappointing.

"Yeah, that's the soonest."

If that's the soonest, what else can I do? I swallow. "How much?"

He shuffles around again. "Based on milage. You're about 75 miles out. Couple hundred."

Couple *hundred*. I should have room on my credit card. I haven't had a paycheck since before the holidays, and now won't get one for at least two weeks.

"So where you want me to take it?" he asks.

"What do you mean?"

He chuckles again. "You want it fixed? Or you just want it at your house?"

"Do you have any recommendations?"

He sounds like he's lighting a cigarette. "Mitch's Garage. On Birch."

"He's a good guy?"

"Yeah, he's pretty good."

"I don't want anyone to take advantage of me," I say.

"I'll tow it there," he says. "Expect it Tuesday. I'll call you with the final bill. And if you end up not paying it, we keep the car."

"I have stuff in the car I need. Can I go pick it up Tuesday?"

"You'll have to call Mitch about that."

He hangs up. I stand up and empty my backpack. Put my CDs away. I go into my closet and move my clothes around so there's a free rack. I open my dresser drawers and clear two of them. My mom can sleep in here. I'll sleep on the couch. We'll figure it out.

The doorbell rings. I go back into the living room. Daniel is standing there talking to Rebecca. He smiles when he sees me.

"You ready?" he asks.

Rebecca pulls her hat on. She turns to me, sticks her tongue in her cheek and backs out, but I pretend she's being normal and don't react.

"Can we stop for cigarettes?" I ask.

He holds a pack of Camel Lights up. "One step ahead of you."

*

Daniel turns onto a street full of large, bare trees. Brick houses. Brown lawns, happy mailboxes. Sophisticated sidewalks. I think of my mother's wandering career as a secretary. She was a secretary before we left Wisconsin. Now, she's a secretary at the company where my stepdad works. That's how they met. They have good insurance, she always tells me. She and my stepdad live in a nice house, but it's small, on the west side of town, and it's old and has a lot of plumbing and roof issues. This neighborhood is where people who make good choices, live good lives, earn good livings live.

Daniel pulls alongside the house and puts the car in park. "You know, I've known you for almost three years, and I've never even met your mom. You've met my parents. Twice."

"She's coming for my birthday," I say.

"Right. To live."

Briefly glancing at him before getting out of the car, I catch him smiling at me—genuinely smiling—and I look away.

The grass is crunchy with that light dusting of snow and frozen, dormant grass. The garage door is open and music wafts out.

In the garage, a space heater hums along. Pieces of art hang on the walls, mostly recognizable paintings of flowers and fruit. A sheet hangs over a large piece mounted toward the back, so I peel a corner back. It's a mirror. A white-haired woman bustles toward us. Maybe the mirror is hers, and she doesn't want anyone to make an offer on it. Or maybe she just doesn't want to look at herself anymore. A stocky black and white dog with cropped ears and a long tongue follows the woman. The dog stops when she stops and then sits at her feet, looking up at me, panting-smiling.

"Welcome, welcome, brave souls," she says, folding her hands as in prayer. All her silver bracelets knock together and sound like wind chimes. "When the weather is nicer, I'll spread out into the backyard."

She's talking to us as though we're coming back after a break in a conversation. She winks at me like I'm in on her secret. The woman is petite, like my mom, and her hair is cropped short and styled. Hair that announces attention to detail. Her make-up is delicate, not too showy, not too cakey, but complimentary and enhancing. When she smiles, the skin around her mouth and eyes create deep lines, but her skin looks well-kept. Her clothes are loose and flowing. A billowy yellow cotton blouse under a heavy, wool gray cardigan is weighted against her chest with a thick silver necklace. Music comes from a CD player she's plugged into the wall. It sounds like the top 40 from the1950s.

"This is Gracie," the woman says in a big, confident, full voice, and the dog wags her tail. "I'm Aurora. I'm so glad you're here today. Do you have items or are you just browsing?"

Daniel steps forward and offers his hand. "Just browsing."

"You're from Hadley's," she says. "I'm glad I was pushy enough to finally get you over here. And this is your girlfriend?"

"I'm not—"

"I'm Daniel," he interrupts and reaches out to shake her hand. "This is Shannon, my best friend."

41

Something about the way he says best friend tugs at me. Smiling her big smile, she welcomes us and encourages us to walk around and see what we can see.

The table in front of us is draped in a black velvet cloth. Necklaces and bracelets form lines from one end to the other. I pick up a silver bracelet and hold it up to the light. It's simple, nothing exciting, but there's a very small charm at the end of it, a cursive e, and I don't know what that e means, if it means "everything" or if it means "essential" or if it was someone's name, like "Emily," but I like it. It makes me happy to look at it. I drape it over my wrist and try to clasp it, but it's awkward to do one-handed, and here's Daniel, taking his gloves off so he can hook the hooks for me.

"Thanks," I say.

"My pleasure," he replies.

"What do you think this is about?" I ask. "What's the story here?"

"Probably some poor bastard gave it to a girl, and she didn't like it," he says.

"Cynic," I reply.

"You are," he says.

I expected crap, the way garage sales are supposed to look. Instead, I see a nice dresser, painted light blue, in the corner. Daniel squats down to look at books. I hear a car door and have to lift my arm to block the sun which has made a surprise visit, the small e dangling off my wrist.

"What makes this an emotional garage sale?" I whisper to Daniel. "It looks like a regular garage sale."

Daniel shrugs. Two older women in parkas walk up the drive. We're not the only fools out today. I lower my hand.

"You should get that," Daniel says.

"No," I say. "It's too expensive."

"That looks gorgeous on you," Aurora says, coming up behind me. The moment is broken, and I take off the bracelet.

The alcohol dried me up last night. The coffee wet me down but not enough.

"May I have a glass of water?" I ask.

I'd hoped she would just point to a cooler—I thought everyone had a cooler in their garage—but she takes my hand. "Come, come."

The door to the house is like my old garage door from the house I grew up in, all scuffed and beaten because it's the most used door in the house. The neighborhood, the lawns, the almost Midwest feel to the place, almost makes me expect to walk into my old mudroom and see laundry baskets, a pile of shoes, a washer and a dryer, the closet where we once had a mouse infestation. But the space is wide and open, Spanish style tile, a long Southwest-inspired rug running into the kitchen, which doesn't reveal my mom at the table, paying bills, waiting on my dad, calling around for my dad, taking her cigarettes and going into the basement for hours and hours, until my dad came home.

Aurora's kitchen is stuffed with knickknacks. My mom is not a knick-knacker. Beanie babies—mostly dogs—line the ledge of the sink. They are in cases. The burners have black and white checkered knitted covers over them. Colored tea towels hang out of every drawer. She opens a pink refrigerator and takes out a pitcher of ice water. She removes a plain glass from the cupboard and pours. The kitchen attaches to the dining room where I see a large dining room table that looks as though it's set for a dinner party.

She passes me the glass of water and stands there as I drink it. A mirror hangs on the wall behind her, and I can see my reflection. I look tired and overwrought, almost drugged and on the side of ragged. The dog plops down at my feet and puts her head on the ground as if she's decided to be sad right along with me.

"I like your house," I say.

Do I? It's a thing to say.

"My husband and I built it together, God rest his soul." She looks up and smiles.

43

"My parents built our old house," I say. "Or, you know, they designed it. They themselves didn't physically build it. Back in the 70s."

"My husband was a carpenter. Let me show you something," she says.

I set my water on a wicker coaster on the counter and follow. She leads me down a bright hall lined with framed color photographs of her and her husband and their kids, three girls. All apparently grown now. Toward the end of the hall, she's framed a picture of Gracie that looks like it was taken in a studio. She's sitting in front of a sky blue back-drop, and her head is cocked slight to the right. Gracie looks like she's smiling.

Aurora veers off to the right, and we enter a large den, lined top to bottom with smooth wooden bookshelves. A section in the middle looks like someone started (and then stopped midway through) carving designs, like tribal tattoos. I reach out to touch it, but pull back.

"Go ahead," she says. "My Jack built these for us." She touches the carvings.

My fingers crawl along the movement in the warm wood. Natural, unperfect grooves exist along the top.

"He died just last summer," she says.

I wait for her to smile to heaven, but she doesn't, and that pleases me. I like people who say die instead of pass. She gazes at the shelves and at the books on them. I don't recognize many of the titles. Daniel might. Has too much time passed for me to say sorry? Sorry your husband died. Sorry for everything. I say nothing.

"That's what really inspired me to do this sale," she says. "I just had all of this stuff." Her voice remains steady, strong. "His clothes and everything, sure, but also cufflinks and bottles he collected and physical things he touched and wore close to his body. It means something to me, but at some point, you have to let go, give it new life. You have to sweep out the old inventory. My friends told me to have a garage

44

sale, get rid of it so I can move on, but I thought, *a garage sale*. I can't have a *garage sale* after forty-two years of marriage. How terribly uninspiring. And was I the only one who thought that way? Surely not." She rubs the wood as if she's trying to conjure Jack himself. "Jack was an artist. He built these shelves because he wanted to create a home for our books." With a catch in her voice, she adds, "He didn't quite get a chance to finish it."

Everything ends. Love. Marriage. Families. Bookshelves.

A gray photo of a barrel-chested man and a curvy woman on the beach sits on the shelf nearest to me. His chest is shiny, reflecting the sun, and the woman's hair is curled and pinned. Her bathing suit is a halter top with a bottom that almost looks like a mini-skirt.

"Is this you?" I ask, pointing.

"And my Jack, my husband."

"You look like a model."

She laughs now, a big, blustery sound that breaks up the devastation the room. "Oh, honey."

My parents were high school sweethearts. Their senior pictures hung next to each other in the family room. My mom's hair was dark and long and parted equally on both sides. She wore make-up back then, her eyes dark and smoky. My dad's hair was long and curly. When I was young, the morning we drove away from our house and my father, who I never saw again, she told me that the kind of love she had for my dad was the difficult kind. She did not ask me what I wanted, or how I felt. I was 8. You don't get much of a say when you're 8. We drove out of the Midwest, and didn't stop until we hit the desert.

"My parents don't like each other," I say.

The photographs in my mom and stepdad's house are of them at the casinos my stepdad likes to go to. She doesn't smile in pictures, just tilts her chin up and looks straight ahead. I don't know what happened to them, those senior pictures—if my dad has them or if my mom took them or if she threw them away. I'll never see my mother young again.

Gracie sighs.

"She likes you," Aurora says.

"What kind of dog is she?" I bend down to pet her, which she acknowledges by thumping her tail on the floor.

"She's a pit bull." Aurora bends down with me and pats her on the back. "Gracie Pants. I got her at the pound when Jack first became ill. She's been with me through all of it. She's my best friend now." Aurora reaches out and touches my arm. "I'm sorry about your parents, honey."

"Oh my God, no. It was forever ago," I say, putting my hand through my hair. "No, no, don't be sorry about that."

She gives me a sad look, and I've been inside too long. We walk outside together.

"Do you take old cars that don't run?" I ask, half-joking.

Her answer is a short laugh. I find Daniel holding a small green tiled lamp. Some of the tiles are missing revealing black, empty spaces. Even though I drank all that water, I'm still thirsty. I haven't gone to the bathroom in hours.

"Where did you go?" Daniel asks.

"I needed something," I say.

"What?"

"A glass of water."

"I like this," he says, holding the lamp to me. "What do you think? I don't see a price."

"You're not considering buying that, are you?"

"I like green. I like this lamp."

"It's hideous. It's missing pieces."

He twirls it around and it sparkles in the sun and soon I can't see him anymore, just his hands holding the lamp.

"That's what I like about it." He taps it. "I don't see the emotional price here." He looks around for Aurora.

The green and yellow spots aren't gone yet. My world is full of flashing polka-dots. "Seriously. You shouldn't buy that," I say.

"Why not?"

"It could be possessed. Like the last person who owned it got murdered or something. Also, it's ugly."

"Beholder," he says. "And I am beholding it. And I do not think it's ugly."

"It's cracked on the bottom. It probably doesn't even work."

"Lalala, I'm going to talk to Aurora," he says, and walks away without giving me a chance to respond.

"I'll wait here," I say.

I find some shade under a tree and lean against it, grateful for the feeling of external support. What would I sell here? Movie stubs, Honey Brown bottle caps, a bottle of Sky vodka, that conversation we had over the hood of my car in the parking lot, a pair of Tevas, that Leprechaun costume, the smell of mint gum mixed with cigarettes, Swisher Sweets, Red Vines, the gas I spent to get to the airport, the Boy Scout Jamboree t-shirt, the pin with the lighting bolt, that Dave Matthews Band song.

I turn my attention to the street where a new car has pulled up. A girl gets out. She's young, like us. She gets a box out of the back seat and walks up the driveway.

Daniel has his wallet out now, and the exchange is made. He walks toward me, proudly holding the lamp. I leave the sanctuary of the tree and fall into step with him, his head in the perfect position to block the sun.

I get in the car as he situates the lamp in the trunk. When he gets in, he reaches into his pocket and holds the bracelet out to me. My mouth drops open.

"Happy birthday," he says.

I start to protest.

"Give me your wrist."

He picks up my wrist and puts the bracelet on.

"Goddamn it, Daniel," I say.

"That's Shannon-speak for 'thank you,' so I'll take it," he says.

"What would you sell at an emotional garage sale?" he asks.

"Nothing," I say.

He pulls out onto the main street. I point up ahead to Target. He nods.

"What about you?" I ask.

"Hadley's," he says and smiles a little.

CHAPTER 4

I am outside in my pajamas, and my mother is on the other end of the phone singing: "Happy birthday, dear Shannon....happy birthday to you!"

"Thank you," I say and exhale smoke.

"How was your first week of classes?" she asks.

She's cheerful. My stepdad is either next to her or listening in on the phone in their bedroom.

"Good," I say, matching her enthusiasm for his benefit. I test my theory. "How is Bill doing?"

This motherfucker can't let anyone live. I can hear him breathing on the line, but I have to pretend he's not there, and my mom has to pretend he's not there.

"He's well, yes, thank you for asking."

Rebecca pops her head out the front door. Holds up a bottle of Baileys. Shakes it at me.

"What are your plans tonight?" she asks.

"Dinner with friends," I say. I hold up a finger to Rebecca. "I—"

I catch myself. I almost said I'll see you in a few days, but, see above, Bill's listening. Bill is always listening. I finish the cigarette. Put it out in the ashtray.

"All right, so I'll see you later," I say. "Thank you for calling."

"Love you, honey," she says. "See you later!"

I hope my mother will hang on a minute so can I tell her I can't wait to see her, but she's gone as well. I've cleared space. Daniel took me to Mitch's garage, and I collected all the garbage bags. Some guy—Mitch maybe—was like, it's the alternator and the something else and the belt needs to be replaced, also you don't have any freon, and the filters are bad, and the tires need air, and on and on. This car just has a bunch of issues, I said to the guy. Sounds like you just got out of a psych class, he said. It wasn't funny, but I laughed.

Daniel and I hauled the bags into my apartment, and I unpacked for her. Hung her blouses. Folded her pants. Clothes she'd been buying with cash the last few months. A coat. Boots. Gloves. Scarf. Completely different climate up here. A few personal items. Some photos of her parents she'd had stored in a box. The rest of it? She was leaving. Fresh start. Brand new June on the horizon.

See you later means goodbye. You can't say goodbye to Bill. His first wife said the words "goodbye" to him, got in her car, drove away and then off a bridge. So says Bill. He's a liar, though, so who really knows. He divorced his second wife, I believe. Anyway. If you say "goodbye" to Bill, it means you're leaving him and his fragile ego shatters, so we all have to say see you later.

Rebecca hands me a cup of coffee filled with Bailey's. "21, bitch," she says.

We clink mugs.

Phone rings again. It's Daniel, not Andy. Thought maybe it would be Andy, but I guess it's too early to be Andy.

"Happy birthday," Daniel says. "I'll see you tonight."

Rebecca and I drink half a bottle of Bailey's before she says she has shit to get done before we go out. I tell her I'm going to hang out in my room. The phone rings again. It's Mitch's Garage. My car will be ready Monday morning. I say I have class. He says yeah, whatever, come after. He says it will $938. The towing cost me about $400. I can swing it, but my card will be fucked. Absolutely maxed out. Happy birthday to me. I move on from the Bailey's. Pour a shot of vodka. Notice the stack of mail on the counter. Credit card bill. No. New credit card offer. Huh. I open it. They're offering me a new line up to $3,000. No interest for six months. Maybe it's the alcohol. Or maybe it's financial salvation. For one single second, I am happy. I fill out the paper, put it in their envelope they provided, and walk to the mailboxes to drop it off.

Back in my apartment, no call from Andy. That's fine. I busy myself. I open a few folders. Look at assignments coming up. Open one of my books. Read a half page then close the book. Fuck it. I dial Andy's number, but no answer. I don't leave a message. I go back to my book. Read another half a page. Get up, go smoke a cigarette. Come back in. Andy called? No, Andy didn't call. I know he knows it's my birthday. He does, right? I told him, probably, 18 times over break. I told him the night before I left. Soon, I'll be 21. We can go to the bars together. Won't that make you happy? We can go out as a real couple. Rebecca knocks on my door. Wants to know if I want to hit Quiznos for lunch. Her treat. Fine, yes.

Rebecca blathers on about something. She has a ride for us tonight. She has a guy for me tonight if I want one. No, thank you. I break down over the sandwich. Tell her that Andy hasn't called me. She pretends to listen. She eats a Baked Lays and watches a cute guy order a sandwich. She tucks hair behind her ear.

"Yeah, dump that guy," she says and then moves on.

When we get back, I rush to the machine. No Andy. No missed calls. I smoke a cigarette, try to replace one addiction with another. Rebecca pops her head outside. Can she borrow my dark jeans?

I look down.

"The ones I'm wearing?"

She raises her eyebrow. "I mean, I think they're a little tight on you."

"I'm wearing these jeans tonight," I say.

She huffs.

I go inside, open a beer even though I hate beer and Rebecca hates beer, and I'm not totally sure why we have this in the fridge. Fuck it. I call Andy again. This time, I leave a message in my best sober voice.

"Hey, so, it's Shannon. Today is my birthday. I'm drinking a beer right now. We're about to go out. Thought I'd call. We're going out for my birthday. To a bar. I'm so excited. Give me a call. Ok, bye."

I hang up and sip the beer, which is absolutely disgusting and I hate it, and stare at the phone until Rebecca yells from across the apartment our ride is here. I swallow it all down in one big chug.

*

Rebecca and I get into the backseat of an Escalade behind a guy who's talking fast and probably high on coke. Some girl who was already in the car—and I forget her name—says he isn't high on coke, he just sells coke. Rebecca says that anyone who sells coke is usually high on coke. He has a gut and eye bags, and he looks like he sells used cars, not coke. Most of the conversation is done via gesturing because Limp Bizkit is so loud. Doing coke is mimed by us rubbing our noses. Selling coke is mimed by shelling out cash, though shelling out cash looks a lot like dealing a hand of poker.

This guy is a friend of Gary's, who Rebecca says was nice enough to give us a ride downtown, so we don't have to drive drunk later. He doesn't have a job and lives in Forest Village, which is full of college kids like us because the management doesn't run credit checks. He seems to like Rebecca's friend Megan, who has somehow ended up with us tonight, who looks like a pixie in a dark gray sparkly sweater and helped herself to the front seat. Megan likes coke. I don't like Megan.

Megan flips around. Her mouth is hanging open, and she starts giggling. "You guys," she says. She pinches her own cheeks. She twists her black rhinestone earring. "I am *wasted*."

The girl that doesn't have a name reaches out and pets Megan on the head. She's her roommate. Or her cousin. Or something. Then she props her feet up on the console. She's wearing a pair of stunning leather boots, plum-colored and brand new.

"I like your boots," I say to her.

She acts like this is a given. She has a big, black mane of hair that she tosses over alternating shoulders as she speaks. "Thanks," she says. "They were a Christmas gift from my parents." She doesn't even look at me when she says it. Then she takes her feet down.

I put my feet up in her place. I'm wearing a pair of dark red heels that I bought from a basement on 3rd street downtown that sells overstocked, slightly damaged, vaguely out of season designer shoes for super cheap. I've been waiting for someone to notice them.

The girl without a name takes a CoverGirl compact out of her purse, opens it, and reapplies powder to her chin and t-zone. "God," she says. "I have to get laid tonight. I'm serious."

Our driver drops us in front of Mad-I, a little dive that sits on the fringe of all the nice, clean bars. It's a cheap place to drink, and there are generally not a lot of douche bags hanging around. There are drunks. There are people too involved in their own misery, but there are no douche bags.

"Great job on the ride," I tell Rebecca as we both dig around in our bags for our IDs, mine specifically, newly minted over 21.

"Hey," she says, "we didn't have to pay for a cab."

"We're lucky he didn't take us into the woods and cut us up," I say.

The girl with no name links arms with Megan. They sashay ahead of us into bar.

"You're the most dramatic person I know," Rebecca says.

While we're waiting to get carded, Rebecca asks, "Where's Daniel?"

"He gets off work late, so I don't know."

"You don't know what?"

"If he's coming."

"If he's coming. Jesus Christ. Daniel missing your twenty-first birthday? I doubt it."

The bouncer eyes me up and down, studies my ID. He lets me in. We sit down inside and a waitress in small shorts and a dirty white wife-beater over a red bra that is too small for her takes our order. Rebecca gets us some screwdrivers, and when the server asks us if we want to start a tab, Rebecca says yes.

Rebecca looks at me in my thin white sweater. She says, "You're going to freeze later."

"I'll just have to drink more," I say.

"Where do you think Megan went?" Rebecca asks.

Megan is the emotional breakdown kind of drunk. She's the girl sitting in a locked stall sobbing about a 10-year-old trauma. She's the girl curled up in the backseat of your car with her thumb in her mouth. She's the kind of girl I can't deal with.

"Maybe she went home," I say. Actually, I'd seen her at the bar a few minutes ago talking to a guy who looked older than Gary.

Rebecca stands on her tiptoes and looks around but then gives up after less than a minute. "Oh well," she says. "She's a big girl. She can take care of herself."

A server shows up with two drinks. We look around. Two guys in white button-down shirts sent them to us. They raise their glasses. Rebecca turns to me. "No, they're gross," she says then slams her drink and nods for me to do the same. "Let's get out of here."

On our way outside, another group of guys gather around us and announce they're going to Fillies. Rebecca says fine, we'll go to Fillies. The booze is hitting. We're in the crosswalk, and I hear music.

"Do you hear that? Rebecca? Do you hear a fiddle?"

Rebecca isn't listening to me; she's talking. It must be coming out of one of the doorways up ahead. Some guy is trying to walk with me. We pass Myth. I once bought a card in there for Adrian that had a picture of a geisha on the front. Inside it said: Haha. You're bisexual.

Tonight, in the window, is a giant poster of Frank Sinatra leaning against a wall, looking out into the nothing with a cocky non-grin on his face and a drink dangling in his right hand. It seems like a thing that exists only for you to covet, a thing you're not supposed to touch. It's a thing you see when you close your eyes at night and imagine the life you really want to be living.

This guy asks, "Are you uncomfortable?"

"No. Why?"

"You're walking with your arms crossed," he says.

"I'm cold."

He takes off his bomber jacket and drapes it around my shoulders. I am immediately warm. Immediately grateful. He seems embarrassed by his own gesture, and I find this incredibly appealing. I walk closer to him.

"Thanks," I say.

"I'm Kevin," he says.

Kevin is tall with floppy brown hair and a medium-to-lightly-interesting smile. I reach into my purse for a cigarette, put it between my lips. Kevin stops me, lights it with a Zippo that he slips into his pocket.

"Shannon," I say as I exhale smoke.

He picks up my hand and winks at me. Winkers seem old-fashioned. Rebecca is taking out her ID to show to the bouncer at Fillies. Kevin's two friends are doing the same. Kevin reaches under his jacket I'm still wearing and hooks a finger into the back pocket of my jeans. He looks coy as he does this. But he only holds it for a moment because the bouncer asks for his ID. Then it's my turn. I smile. Try to hold myself steady. The guy lowers it and looks at me. He lets me in but in a way that says he doesn't want to.

"Where did you get that jacket?" Rebecca asks. She looks me over. "It's hideous."

"That guy," I say, gesturing to Kevin & Co., who've managed to get a booth in the middle of a crowded bar on a Friday night. An impressive feat.

She leans forward and says something to the bartender and seconds later we have two light red shots in front of us.

"Cheers," she says. "To guys with ugly coats."

We shoot the shots. She leans forward and says something else to the bartender.

I watch the bartender make our drinks. Glass. Ice. Booze, booze, fountain spray thing, garnish, straw. Go.

Rebecca pushes through people like it's her full-time job. I'm behind. I make eye contact with a guy standing in the middle of the floor, and he smiles at me. With this jacket on, I feel marked.

Frat boys line the walls. In a striking turn of events, they also have on white button shirts. They are all smoking, but they don't even know the right way to smoke. They hold the cigarette between their fingers like a joint. A few girls are dressed like me. Gauzy sweater. Jeans. This makes me feel bad about myself. So I drink more.

Fillies is gamey, full of sweaty bodies and heat. It's very loud. It's like being in that Escalade only it's not crappy Limp Bizkit we're listening to, it's Quad City DJs.

There is no room to actually sit in the booth, the boys have occupied it to the fullest extent, so Rebecca and I stand in front of it while getting bumped by people walking past us. When the guys go by, they put their hands on us, trying to get a cheap feel. A girl bumps into Rebecca, spilling her drink down her arm, and barely says sorry.

Kevin gets out of the booth. He takes the empty glasses to the bar. Then he snuggles up to me, starts talking, does a lot of gesturing with his hands. He laughs. So I laugh, because I like fitting in. I smile and shake my head in an agreeable way, even though I don't have any idea what he's saying. I lean closer and as I do, one of the guys from Mad-I who sent Rebecca and I drinks wanders by, looks me up and down and then calls out, "Slut!" and keeps going.

Kevin doesn't notice, or if he does, he pretends not to.

"Fires!" Kevin yells over the music. "I am a firefighter! In the forest! When there are fires in the forest, I go out there!"

The bass in the sound system digs a hole in my chest.

"I'm a Hotshot!" he yells.

Rebecca dances by herself. I tap her on the shoulder and then point to the Adrians coming through the crowd. He's gotten a hair cut. She has too. They've cut their hair in the exact same way. A spiky mullet thing I've been seeing on the teenagers who hang out in front of the mall.

Adrian reaches for me, gives me a good solid hug. It is so tight, so intimate I pull back and look up into his eyes. Red and glassy. He's high. But he puts his mouth against my ear. Tells me happy birthday, tells me I look good. This sends a heat wave through my body. Unexpected but I'll take it. Daniel is right behind him. Kevin hovers.

"You're off early," I say to Daniel.

"We were slow," he says.

I put my hands in Kevin's pockets and find a pack of cigarettes and the Zippo. Firefighters shouldn't smoke. The Zippo is black with a horse or something on the front. The cigarettes are not my brand. I don't care. The need for a cigarette is killing me. I screw the cigarette into my mouth and attempt to ignite the Zippo. Kevin the Hotshot takes the Zippo from my fingers. He flicks it, and a flame erupts. I lean toward him. Grateful, I mouth *thank you* to him. He smiles.

Kevin the Hotshot postures over me now, so I have to introduce them, which is difficult over the noise and heat of the packed bar.

"This is my friend Daniel," I say to Kevin.

"Nice to meet you, man," Kevin says.

"He's a Hotshot," I say, trying to be helpful.

"A what?" Daniel asks.

"Is this your boyfriend?" Kevin asks in my ear, with what I think is genuine concern.

"No," I say.

"Is that other guy your boyfriend?" he asks.

"No," I say.

"Do you have a boyfriend?"

Andy. I think about Andy. Sometimes I call Andy my boyfriend. Not in front of Andy. In, like, a casual way. Like, I'll tell some stranger Andy is my boyfriend if I know that person has no way of knowing Andy. There might be a message on my machine. I also think about how the last time I talked to Andy, I was stuck at Love's with a broken down car and he never called to see if I was ok. To be fair, I didn't call him to tell him, either. He wants to be left alone. I can deal with that as long as sometimes—you know, just once in awhile, he gives me what I need from him: pure, focused attention.

Kevin though. He leans in and says very carefully, "You're too pretty not to have a boyfriend."

Oh my god. Dying. I'm dying. I've died. Daniel looks from him to me, and I give Daniel a short, affirmative nod, and he disappears into the crowd, probably off to find some beer. Time has a funny way of changing when you're drunk. It moves in a different way. It can go faster or slower or however you want it to go. Or else sometimes it completely disappears. Our drinks come out fast and we drink them fast, and the table piles up with empty glasses, which Kevin continues to clear off.

Adrienne is rolling around in the booth completely fucked out of her mind. Adrian the boy is chain-smoking cigarettes and sitting up with his arms spread across the back of the booth like he's a king. He's smiling, and I know that he only smiles like that, with his eyes, when he's obliterated. Rebecca takes my arm and pulls on it. She turns me to face her and opens her eyes wide.

"What?"

She leans in and shouts/whispers. "Look what she's doing. But be casual. Do not draw attention."

I pretend the lighter I'm using doesn't work so that I have to turn around and face the booth to get the matches off the table. Adrian, with his arms still spread out, has his eyes closed and his mouth hanging open. I see the top of Adrienne's head in his lap and –

I turn back to Rebecca. "Oh my God," I say. "Are you kidding me?"

But I am a little jealous. I glance back over at them, try not to stare. Rebecca shakes my arm.

"What's with the coat guy?"

"He's nice," I say. "He's a forest firefighter. A Hotshot."

"He told you he was a Hotshot?"

"Yeah." I look over at Kevin who is looking at me and wave at him. He starts to approach.

"That's douchy," she says, sipping her drink.

"It is not. When you meet people, you tell them what you do."

"And where, praytell, are these forest fires he fights? Hasn't been a fire here in twenty years."

Kevin pulls on my arm. He wants me to dance with him. I let Kevin take me. For god's sake, someone has to want me tonight. Daniel is hanging out by himself now looking at his watch nursing whiskey. Kevin kisses me with a hard mouth, which I wasn't sure I expected so soon, then puts his hands, ice-cold, under my shirt.

Rebecca is next to us. She takes my arm. "We're leaving."

I look at Kevin, and then back at her. "We just got here."

"Karaoke is starting.

"I have to go to the bathroom."

"In *Fillies*? Are you out of your mind?"

I take off the jacket, give it back to Kevin. See you later, I tell him and pat him on the chest. On our way to the Icehouse, we cut through the park so I can pee because I'm going to explode. Rebecca promises me if she sees anyone coming, she'll yell. On my way out from behind the bushes I trip but throw myself farther away so I don't land in my own pee. I wash my hands in the drinking fountain. We start walking back to the main strip of bars.

We catch up with Daniel and Adrian and Adrienne.

"It's you again," Daniel says.

I keep walking, fast, because it's cold and I'm drunk and I've lost my sense of rhythm.

"What?" I ask, annoyed because he's staring at me.

"What happened to the jacket?"

"I gave it back."

"Does he fight fires in that jacket?

"What's your problem?"

"I'm a Hotshot," Daniel says in a deep voice. "I'll make you a fire."

"Hotshots put out fires."

"Whatever."

"He was nice to me, which is a good change from what I usually deal with."

We get caught up in a crowd going into the Icehouse, which is where drinks are expensive and the music usually sucks (case in point, they're doing bar karaoke tonight) so it's no surprise to me to see our driver sitting at a table with Megan and the girl with the fucking fabulous pair of boots. I want. I want those boots. Megan is smoking and looking like she's got nothing in her head but vapors. As we get closer, I notice the guy's hand doing something to Megan that is inappropriate and wrong for public.

Rebecca says, "What in the holy hell is wrong with the world tonight?"

I don't know, but something has come undone and it's heading straight for us. I'm in that place of alcohol where the things that were feeling nice and even are starting to grow spikes.

Megan sees us and waves so hard she almost falls out of her chair. The sound in my head is someone telling me to cut myself off, but I can't. This is the problem. I can't cut myself off. I'm not a person who cuts myself off. My body will do that for me later when I start throwing up.

Adrian and Adrienne order a round of drinks, and Megan giggles about something. Maybe it's the fact that our driver is an old man hanging out with 21-year-olds. Or maybe it's that we're sitting in the Icehouse.

I've broken the seal. I have to go to the bathroom again and somehow Adrienne and I elect ourselves as buddies and go together. I make a crack about assholes at the Icehouse, and she laughs, which kind of makes me feel good and maybe reassess the idea that she's ruining Adrian's life. She disappears into a stall.

At the sink I wash my hands and look at my drunk, dirty face. What the hell fluorescent lighting? What the hell.

A toilet flushes and this girl with dark hair and a body full of sobriety comes out. She walks a straight line from the stall to the sink, and I awkwardly move out of her way.

"Shannon?" she asks.

I look at her, but then have to put my hands on the sink to get steady. The sink is wet. The sink in here is always wet.

"Oh hey," I say. "Hey."

We met freshman year. We had a psych class together and then, like, ended up in a bunch of psych classes sophomore year, too. We were supposed to move up to abnormal together, but we didn't. A scheduling glitch kicked me out. When I registered last April, I wasn't paying attention and put myself in two classes at once. Abnormal Psych and this one I'm in now, European history that mostly involves The Black Death. Not so much a glitch then but more like an avoidable mistake. When I talked to the psych professor about an override, he asked me to explain why I wanted to take his class. I said I liked psychology. He asked me why. I tried to say it seemed like a way to find out some things about myself. He took my rambling as a non-answer and said he understood if I couldn't explain on the spot. I could think about it, then I could write it out, get it back to him in a day or two. Then he'd sign the override. I walked out of his office very clear on one thing. I'd stick with history, because history didn't need me to write some self-affirming bullshit paper about it.

"I wondered what happened to you," she says.

What the hell is Adrienne doing? Is she dead? I crouch down, lose my balance and reach out to use the sink to steady myself, then try to act as though I meant to do that. When I stand, I feel like it's not me that's standing. It's some weird floating version of me. I take the sink again. That girl can probably use me as a case study for her psychology class. She should be taking notes. I reach into my pocket to see if I have a pen and some paper, but I don't.

"Anyway, though, I couldn't get in, so I just let go," and as I say that, I actually let go and sort of stumble back and have to grab onto the towel dispenser.

The toilet flushes. I can't believe how white it is in this bathroom. Everything shines. It's shiny and sparkly like we're in an ad for Pinesol. Maybe this is supposed to be an igloo. This bathroom is what the rest of the Icehouse should be, if the Icehouse was a real icehouse.

"Well, I'm pretty messed up," I say.

This last part comes out on accident. I had not intended for it to come out at all, but there it is. I am messed up. Things are messed up. Adrienne is not my friend. My mouth is numb.

"Oh," she says.

It's like she wants to say more, but doesn't know what more there is to say. She's wavering in and out of my line of vision. Sometimes she's there and sometimes she's not. She's Synergy. Show's over.

Adrienne crashes out of the stall and stumbles up to me. She's sniffing and wiping her nose. My old friend here looks at Adrienne with such pure intrigue I am caught up in it and feel my body start to shift down like maybe we're going to study her together, and it's not me who's the fucked up main

Stephanie Austin

character. Adrienne sways and bumps into me and then knocks into the sink.

She whispers loudly, "I left some in there."

The bathroom door opens and Adrian the boy comes in. He sees me, but doesn't see me and I wave at him like I'm flagging down a car. He stops and takes out a Sharpie and begins drawing on the front of one of the stalls. Um, I say. But then he wanders into the stall with the drugs. And I think the last place Adrian needs to be is in a woman's bathroom stall with drugs.

He made a cursive Q, which is really the number two. Such a racket, letters and numbers. I'm starting to feel sick, like throw-up sick. I'm starting to feel tired and depressed and sad again. Adrian stumbles out of the stall, falls into me.

"I can't do it anymore," he says.

"What is it?"

"All of it?"

"What the fuck does that mean? Are you suicidal or something?"

"No, I'm releasing," he says.

The middle of the night is the best time to say out loud how awful you feel, how sad you are because the whole world is sad, and how we're all drowning in each other. I slide onto the tile floor with Adrian and don't think I'll be able to get up. But we do.

Something is wet. It's me. The water from the sink is all over me.

Adrienne is trying to get a paper towel and she's having a hard time. "Let's go," she says not to me but to the paper towel dispenser.

When we get back to the table, there's shots waiting for us. Blow Jobs. Kahlua and whipped cream.

You can't use your hands. I attempt to get my mouth around the rim, make eye contact. "I can't get it," I say.

"Yes you can," Rebecca shouts next to me over the music. She takes my hands and puts them behind my back.

"Oh my god. I've done like a hundred of these. Don't be a wuss about it."

I kind of angle around the shot glass in a different way. Success. Trick is to relax your jaw muscles. Like you're at the dentist. I knock the Blow Job back, the whipped cream mixed with the liquor runs down each side of my face, down the sides of my throat, and I try to catch the drips with my hands before they hit my sweater but fail. The rush of fluid makes me choke. I drop the shot glass from my mouth like a dog dropping a ball. The glass bounces off the table and rolls, but I grab it. And don't look now, but the leader of the fuck brigade has arrived. Here's Gary in his white, button-down shirt and dark jeans, an absolute walking cliché of douchery putting his arms around Rebecca.

"Hey," a voice says pulling me out of the abyss.

He's back. Kevin is back. And he's smiling. He saw the whole thing. Clearly he is impressed with me. I am impressive. Say it like you mean it. I am *impressive.*

CHAPTER 5

Someone is murdering Whitney Houston. White, crusty stains form on my shirt from the whipped cream from the blow job drink. Daniel's on his third or fourth beer. Rebecca goes through the motion of paging through the karaoke song book and pretends to think long and hard about her options. She closes the book. Gary shoves the book across the table at me. No, no, I shake my head. Only Rebecca sings. I light another cigarette.

"Some guy called me a slut," I tell Daniel.

"What?"

"Guy walked by me and yelled out that I was a slut," I say. "I am not a slut."

Gary has his hand down Rebecca's pants. I point to her.

"Rebecca is the slut."

"Rebecca is friendly," Daniel says.

"I'm not a slut," I repeat.

"Who said you were?" Daniel repeats.

Rebecca abruptly claps her hands. Kevin returns to the table with another drink for me. I stand, let Kevin sit, then I sit on his lap and exhale smoke.

"You smoke too much," Gary says to me.

I blow the smoke in his direction. Adrienne combs through Adrian's hair with her greasy fingers.

Kevin holds my hand. This never happens with Andy. Andy does not hold my hand in public. And look at Kevin! Holding my hand! In public! This is why Kevin is good. Andy bad. Kevin good. Daniel by himself. But Daniel is ok. He is ok, I promise.

Our server comes by. Rebecca practically screams at her. "We have a birthday here. It's her 21st birthday."

After I show her my ID, the server says she can get me a free shot. Great. Fantastic. My blood alcohol is alcohol.

Rebecca's name gets called. She prances around and sings *Let's Hear it for the Boy*.

The boy tonight is Gary as Rebecca directs all her attention to him during the song. But, like, here's the thing. Rebecca is a good singer. She was in choir in high school, and she was the lead in musicals. She's a genuinely good singer. Why she studies interior design is beyond me.

"You want to get out of here?" Kevin asks into my ear.

His breath sends my body into a frenzy. A thrilling feat because I thought it was only Andy. Andy has this weird hold over me, but here's Kevin, trying to beak it.

"Where?" I ask.

"I live a block or two from here," he says. "We can go."

I'm not stupid. I'm not getting in a *car* with this guy. Rebecca is flustered from the applause still, I guess. She has her hand to her heart like she can't believe it. The next singer sings *Help!* by the Beatles. Daniel sings along. He loves The Beatles maybe more than he loves anything else.

Rebecca balls her fists in mock rage. "I fucking hate the Beatles," she says.

She hates the Beatles during karaoke because everyone knows every word to every Beatles song ever. So the crowd sings and drowns out the singer thereby negating, according to the Book of Rebecca, the art and beauty of a karaoke singer.

"Wait for me outside," I drip into Kevin's ear. You don't have to tell him twice. He's gone. I slither over to Daniel, who is still happy with *I need somebody, not just anybody*.

I reach into him, which at first he's surprised by but then lifts his arm, like he's been waiting. What I want, though, is in his inner jacket pocket. He lets me while maintaining eye contact. He leans into me, and I remove his keys. His expression changes to confusion. I close my fingers around the keys, lean in. "I kind of need to get out of here," I say.

"You are not sober," Daniel says as I hurry off.

I pretend I don't hear him, disappear into the crowd and out the door where I find Kevin waiting, arms open.

CHAPTER 6

A ROAD CLOSED sign blocks the driveway. Kevin meets me in front of it. I drove with the windows down, the cold air waking me up, and Daniel had a pack of Camel Lights in his glove box with one inside, so I smoked it.

The hotshot lives in a big house in a cul-de-sac. He was right. Wasn't far. = Barely counted as drunk driving.

I ask him about the ROAD CLOSED sign.

"Some crew just left it," he says. "My friends and I move it around to fuck with each other. It's funny when you think about it. A road crew just leaving their shit all over the place."

I don't know if I think that's funny. What is it with guys and construction signs? What do you guys think is so hilarious about them?

I expect his living space to look like a fire station, but it's just a house. No medals on the wall. No Dalmatians in the corner. No trucks in a big garage off to the side. He reaches out for my purse and then tosses it on the back of a chair. We stand facing each other, his left arm casually at his side. He's open and forward, the body language of party. He offers me a drink. I tell him I'll have a water. See? I say to Daniel in my head. See. He pours me a glass of water and then also gives me a shot of tequila and then also offers me a cigarette and lights it with his Zippo.

"To 21," he says.

We shoot the shots, and I gag but try to pretend like I don't. He laughs, but it's not mean.

He's cute. I like the attention. He takes my hand again. Fuck, I love it when they take my hand. Someone cooked on the stove last night, and bits of meat and crumbs and spices are all over the white stovetop. The trash needs to be taken out. The wall behind the stove is yellow-brown.

I feel blurry, a little sick, and he's leading me into the living room. He pulls me on top of him as he sits on a recliner. What I want most of all is for Andy to see me with another guy. For Andy to tell me he loves me back. Kevin's a big guy. His forearms are thick.

"How many fires have you been in?" I ask.

He puts his hands on my legs. "Just controlled burns."

"What happens to animals in a forest fire?"

His mouth is on my neck.

His house smells like guys who sometimes skip showers. The dirty brown recliner we're on is damaged. It doesn't recline. He found it on a curbside and put it in the bed of his pick-up truck. This thing was marked for trash, he tells me. He reaches under my shirt and runs his hands over my bra and underneath my bra and then he unhooks it and tosses it on the floor before I have a chance to react. As he does this, he talks about his hotshot training. Did I ask? They go into the valley in the summer and hike in the heat with all their gear. He's soaking wet when it's all over. Do I know what that feels like? To be soaking wet? My head is swimming into that place it goes, where things feel disconnected but not in a bad way.

The carpet is stained and shredded in places. Dust covers the TV. He turns it on and it's an episode of the Simpsons. I'm more South Park than Simpsons. He laughs way too hard at the Simpsons. Then he kisses me, like, really hard. He flips us around so I'm under him. He's nibbling on my lips, gnawing on my lips and growling. Who does this? Who growls when they're making out with someone? His teeth on my mouth sound distant, like I'm listening to something on the other side of a concrete wall breaking open.

He puts his hand in my hair and pulls. I try to laugh and move, and he sort of acknowledges this over his shoulder but starts again. I try to ask him questions about his life and his goals and if he likes steak or Doritos or Mountain Dew, but he doesn't answer, just continues to pull on my hair and rub against me and chew on my mouth. He pulls back and looks down at me.

"You are so beautiful," he says.

My mouth is throbbing. I stare up at him. Then I start to reach for my bra, but he pins my hands, puts his mouth on my neck and moans and rubs against me. He's hard. He loosens his grip so I think I can stand, and I do, but then he, like, picks me up and carries me into his bedroom and I do not know what to do now.

Mouth is cotton. Head getting spikes. Throat dry. I whisper for another drink. Tequila doesn't solve any of my current problems, but it's wet and it goes down. He takes off his shirt. His chest is muscled. The hiking. The sweat running down his chest, carving it out.

He puts his hand between my legs, and I clench up but that doesn't matter anymore and he laughs a little and pries me open. "Let me feel you," he says. "Don't be like that."

The hotshot paws at my body, ravenous, and he's bigger and stronger than he was five minutes ago. He pulls off my shirt, and I am exposed and reflexively cross my arms over my chest, but he pulls them off and stares at me. His breath is hot, acidic. He has my pants off and then slides off my underwear and I keep my legs clenched. He holds my underwear over me. He inserts a finger, then two. It doesn't feel good, but he thinks it feels good, and somewhere in all this, I understand at least a portion of this is desire and the desire is for me.

Abruptly, he stops, sits up, and wipes his hand on his comforter, and I stare at that spot, brighter than the dark, and I start to shift, to feel around on the floor for my underwear.

"Just the tip," he says, but he lies.

I am frozen. Stunned.

He doesn't look at me, so I don't look at him, and I feel the alcohol and his body putting me down, like I'm falling, going under and away, and outside, through the window, I see the moon, and the anesthesiologist said, "This won't hurt. You won't feel anything."

He inserted an IV. My mom sat near me. She held my hand, brushed the hair off my face, and told the man I wanted to be a doctor when I grew up. He asked me if that was true, and I said I didn't know, which felt like the wrong answer. I was 11. Getting my tonsils removed because of chronic ear infections. Bill sat next to my mom. He asked the doctor where he could go smoke, then told my mom he wanted her to come with him. Then she left me.

The tonsil nurse said she liked my hair. Pretty auburn hair. People pay a lot of money for hair like yours, honey.

"If you start counting back from 100," the doctor said, "you'll be out before you hit 50. You'll wake up still you, but you without tonsils."

100. When I came home from the hospital,

99. I stood in the cold hallway,

98. put my cheek against the wall,

97. covered my mouth but still the vomit came.

96. Not vomit, mostly blood

95. down the white walls of our house.

94. My stepfather's house

93. where we moved

92. after living in a motel for a month.

91. His house was loud.

90. Howling outside because

89. he lived next to a wash

88. in the desert.

87. That wind

86. made the windows bang and rattle.

85. So one day,

84. my stepfather came home with a caulking gun.

83. He brought me into my bedroom,

82. opened the curtains.

81. Pointed to the bent trees,

80. pointed to the windows and said,

79. See the gap?
78. He drew a line
77. straight down.
76. Pink junk oozed,
75. slid along the window,
74. sealed it shut.
73. You finish.
72. He took his gun,
71. went into the living room,
70. used the paste to
69. fix the house,
68. all its windows,
67. closed off.
66. All the mascara I wore
65. made me look like a slut.
64. Wanting friends
63. meant I wasn't satisfied with the household.
62. I stayed in my room.
61. My now quiet room.
60. I read Nancy Drew books, listened to Rick Dees
    Weekly Top 40 on my headphones.
59. I didn't show respect to a man
58. who was forced to raise me because
63. my own father was absent,
62. only loved himself.
61. My stepfather
60. did me a kindness, and
58. never left bruises
57. where anyone could see them.
56. He taught me
55. how to caulk.
54. The house
53. became silent.
53. The outside
51. unable to get in.

CHAPTER 7

The hotshot is deflated. The smell of dead ocean hangs above us. Down the hall, I see a slice of white light from the kitchen. He's naked, exposed, his hand over his chest. Not touching me anymore. His chest rises and falls quickly as he's catching his breath. Like after a hike.

He sits up and pats my leg. "That was good. That was so fucking good." Then he pushes himself off the bed and disappears.

I don't shift but the space between us seems to widen. For a long time I stay like this. Quiet. Listening. Burning.

"I need some water," I say.

I sit up. Move now to get my clothes back on my body, move down the hall, get my shoes back on my feet. I should go to the bathroom. Always pee after sex. Don't get an infection.

I rush around collecting my clothing from around his house like a small-town prom queen, and when I bend down to get my purse, I feel the gush of him in my underwear. *Goddamn it*. In the living room, I struggle with my bra. My hands are shaky and my fingers slip. I'll deal with this later. Everything that went off goes back on. The sweater. The purse. His Zippo sits on the counter next to a pack of cigarettes. I take a cigarette. The moment I wrap my fingers around the Zippo, he's up behind me, so I let go.

"What are you doing?" he asks.

"Nothing," I say.

He puts his arms around me and pulls me into him.

Am I slurring? I'm slurring. I brace for him to say I can't leave. You're drunk and you can't go anywhere.

"Man, I'm shot," he says. "Do you want me to walk you to your car?"

Oh. Or that. He's kicking me out.

"No," I say. "No thanks. I got it."

I walk out into the cold. The only light is the light spilling from the house. Daniel's car is parked crooked, an accusation.

Start the car. Put the cigarette in the mouth. Be normal. Push the lighter in and wait. I back up without looking and hit the goddamn ROAD CLOSED sign, lurch forward, turn at the last second and jam my shoulder into the steering wheel after I violently brake. I get out of Daniel's car bracing for damage. How did he—what happened here? He moved it so I could drive through. I see now. He moved it out then back in, like he was opening and closing a gate. The trees and everything obscure the front porch, but he's gone. I walk around the sign trying to figure out what to do. I walk left, then circle back around the right then look back over at the porch then circle again. Stop. It needs to move like four inches to the left and then I can get through. I try to grip the sign itself, but it's awkward. Try again. No give. I look back at the porch. The living room light is off. So I think if I—ok, if I squat and reach to try to get my fingers around the metal stand in the back. Can't quite—almost get it then give up. I let go. Pant. Maybe I just ram the fucking thing.

I think I can shove it with my shoulder. I position myself in the front and put all my weight against it and push, hard then break. If my shoulder wasn't going to bruise before, it will now. I rub it for a second while avoiding looking back at the house.

The bite in the night air feels like an invasion, and the quiet of the trees beyond where I stand is a child's ghost story. I push again, and the sign moves but still not enough. Stop. What was that? Listening. Nothing. Bugs. No, it's too cold for bugs. I push the sign again. Stop. Put my hands on my hips and breathe and feel the dark. The dark is where you put all the terrible things. The monsters. You stuff them in, push them down, push hard, harder, and when they still don't fit, you release a part of yourself down with them because you understand that's the only way to make them stay.

I get back in the car, back out onto the dead grass, get back onto the street and drive home where I stumble in and find Rebecca's door shut this time—blessed be to God—and a body on the couch. I lean over, and it's Daniel. Shit. *Shit.* I stop by the answering machine. No messages from Andy. I set Daniel's keys on the coffee table, hold my breath and tiptoe to my room.

I undress in the dark, empty out my jeans pockets: loose change and receipts.

I sit on the toilet. Relief momentarily takes the place of shame. When I wipe, I expect pain or tenderness, but there's nothing, no feeling but the same feeling I've always felt, which is that it's there. Wash my hands, wash the rest of me, and soon I'm in the shower. It feels better to be clean. After, in my bedroom, I put on my pajamas. I take the bottoms off and settle into bed in my underwear, cover with the blanket. I don't know I'll be able to sleep. I turn to one side, feel my shoulder, a bruise already forming, and then turn back. It's unwieldy, this new injury.

CHAPTER 8

Daniel and Rebecca stop talking when I come out of my room
the next morning. They're on the couch, heads together, then
they zip up. Rebecca eyes me, looks me up and down and
snarls a little, which means she disapproves of something I'm
wearing. It's my freshman year sweatshirt. Says Benton State
across the front. It's gray, yellow, and blue and stained in a
bunch of places.

Daniel. I stole his car. I walk into the kitchen. Pour
myself the last of the coffee. Mostly grounds, but I drink it
straight and when it hits my stomach, my stomach is like hell
no. I dash into the bathroom and slam the door shut and vomit
up everything. All of it comes out. The alcohol, the cigarettes,
the hotshot.

Gasping, I reach for the toilet paper and wipe my
mouth then flush the toilet, sit on the floor of the bathroom.
Absolutely no words for how unbearably awful I feel.

I stand, run some water and splash my face. Purplish
bursts spread like two tiny starfish under each eye. I look
cyanotic, like someone who has drowned.

When I open the door, Daniel is there.

"You all right?" he asks. He thumbs behind him. "I
started a new pot of coffee for you."

"Thanks," I say and push past him. I need a cigarette.
Daniel has a new pack for me. I stick one in my mouth. No
matches. Daniel also has a lighter. An old blue Bic. I pick it up,
flick it. "You want one?" I ask Daniel.

He kicks a rock with the top of his favorite shoe, those
scruffy black and white Chuck Taylors he's had forever.

"What did you get up to last night?" he asks after a
long silence.

"Nothing. What about you?"

"I had to get a ride from Rebecca and her 'friend' Gary
because you took my car."

"I didn't take your car. I just—" I inhale, exhale the smoke. "I had to get out of there."

"You didn't go home though."

Daniel closes the door behind him. Rebecca is in the kitchen, pouring herself more coffee. She twirls her finger next to her hair mouths *curly*. I roll my eyes.

I pour myself a cup but there's no creamer and no sugar. I try to stop myself from screaming. I leave the coffee on the counter, think maybe I'll go across the street to the coffee place but, of course, I don't have a car. I poke through the mail on the counter. No new credit card. I've been giving the guy at the shop a bunch of excuses. Schedule. No ride. Bad weather. That's the obvious lie. The weather this winter has been, well, not pleasant, it's very cold out, but it's been mild. My car's been ready since Friday, but I can't pay for it until this new card shows up. Towing got paid but it ate up all the space on my current card. Daniel follows me into my room.

He plops down at my desk, next to a stack of CDs and starts pawing through them.

"Don't mess those up. I'm bringing those to Hastings to sell."

"Not Steve Miller Band!" he says and holds the disc up.

"Yeah, well, I need gas money."

"When is your car going to be done?" he asks.

"Next week," I lie.

I open my top drawer, thinking my underwear is in there but remember that's the drawer I cleared for my mother. Daniel stops on The Kinks Greatest Hits. He gave that one to me, but he doesn't say anything. My books for spring are stacked next to my CDs. The receipt still sticking out from one of them.

"How are classes going?" Daniel asks.

The casualness of his nicety is a tear in the continuum. My head hurts. My exhaustion is visceral. I need real coffee, not this bullshit. I open my second drawer.

"I sort of miss school," he says. "Maybe I'll go back for a master's degree."

The sound of his voice amplifies the pain in my head.

"I don't know. Creative writing. English Literature. I like school. I like the schedule. Semesters work for me, you know? Just enough time to get in, care about something, then leave again. I really have thought about it. Maybe I'll stay here for another two years. Benton has an M.F.A. program. I have a pile of writing. I might apply and then—"

"Will you please, please, please stop talking?" I say, almost shout, and Daniel recoils, like literally clamps his mouth shut.

That makes me feel shitty. It does. He is wounded, again. I have wounded him, again. It's the same look before winter break. When he asked me—never mind, it doesn't matter. Daniel stands up. Realigns the CDs.

"I'll give you a call in a few hours," he says.

The headache threatens to burst.

"You don't need to call me later, Daniel. I'm fine. I'm a grown up big girl. You don't need to call to check in on me."

He laughs a little. "All right. Happy birthday, Shannon."

He closes the door, softly, behind him and I stand there, fists closed. I take my wallet out of my purse, grab my sunglasses and walk to the coffee shop across the street where I order a mocha, no whip, and the girl behind the counter taps her mouth, says, "you have a little something," but I don't know what she's talking about, so I pay for my drink and while I'm waiting, go into the bathroom and check the mirror. Maybe there's vomit on my cheek or something, but no, I see what she means. My mouth is red, lips a little swollen, a little dark. I press them. They feel like a bruise. I am sucked back into last night. The chewing, the gnawing, the growling. I look closer, press harder until I hurt myself so much I cry.

PART TWO:

Monstrous and Curious Things

CHAPTER 9

Neighborhood Insurance is in a strip mall a block away from campus, sandwiched between a Cartridge World and Stromboli's. I've had this job for a year. 10-15 hours a week. Filing. Answering phones every so often. $7.25 an hour. Not bad, I guess. . When I pull the door open, a bell dings, and Carmen, the pale, thin, raven-haired, straight-banged front desk receptionist who considers herself to be too good for front desk reception, looks up, sees it's me and goes back to clicking her mouse. Today, my mother is coming. Not even Carmen's weird, bad moods will change that.

Poking out from her sleeve, the tip of a cherry, and beyond that, a super severe tattoo on her forearm she showed me once: a large Betty Paige wearing sexy sailor attire holding cherry stems in her left hand while cocking her hip.

We were in the bathroom at the same time and she rolled her sleeves back to wash her hands. She caught me staring. I didn't ask her anything stupid, like, did it hurt? Do you know it's permanent? I said it was cool, because I thought it was cool. I've thought about getting a tattoo, purposefully scarring myself from the outside in. She just smiled, dried her hands and walked out ahead of me.

"Hi," I reply, taking off my hat and coat.

"How's it going?" she asks.

"My mom is coming today," I say.

She glances up, gives me a once over.

"You look tired," she says.

She doesn't say this out of concern. We're not friends. She says it because it's true and she thinks she's clever. She's the kind of person who thinks rudeness is wittiness.

"I am tired," I say, as I go into the office.

"There's some bagels in the back," she says after me.

I pass the row of uniform cubicles and all the shit people stack inside them — dried flowers, glass figurines of children holding balloons, cat calendars, snow globes, vacation photographs—to get to the breakroom, which looks and feels like the inside of an unwashed coffee pot. Two of the senior administrative assistants stand around chatting. The taller one, Marie, is my supervisor, but she didn't hire me. The lead sales guy hired me. I've seen him twice in the last six months. He'll stop by my desk and rub my shoulder, tell me to relax and offer a hope that I'm enjoying my life. Then he'll ask me to scan or email something. Then he'll leave.

Marie, who is covered in beige, is showing off her new shoes, also beige, holding her foot off the floor and wiggling it around, while the shorter one, Nina, turns her head this way and that way as though she's appreciating a good piece of art.

"They look comfortable," Nina says. "Are they comfortable?"

"Oh yes," Marie replies. "They are so comfortable."

She points her toe like a ballet dancer.

"They look versatile," Nina says. "Are they versatile?"

"Oh yes," Marie replies. "I can wear them with anything."

She's talking about a pair of brown loafers with tassels hanging off the top, the kind my mom picked out for me to wear in grade school. Those shoes are nothing more than a cry for help. I take a tight breath and can't let it go.

"You're here early," she says as the two of them walk out together. "Good. I'd like to have a chat with you."

I smile at her in acknowledgment.

"Come to my office when you're done."

Marie pretends to like me because that's what you have to do in the world, pretend to like people until better people come along. I pretend to like her. I pick up a bagel and decide I only want half. The small knife in the sink is covered in damp, white cream cheese, so I open the drawer in front of me and remove the big, serrated one. Because why? Because it's close and not so much effort. Because someone who worked here now or in the past decided an office break room needs a big-ass serrated knife. Picking it up is less effort than washing the small one. I've hardly begun to cut when I feel and hear the sound of the skin on my left pointer finger ripping. I drop the knife and pull my finger away. For a flash of a second it's still just my finger, and I think I didn't even cut myself. I'm fine. I didn't even break any skin. Then, it starts. Blood surfaces from the opening and spills over.

Daniel hates blood. Last summer, we'd all been out, doing what it is we do. Some friends of friends had hooked into our group. At the train tracks, while crossing, one of the girls tripped, fell, and ripped open her hand. I thought Daniel was going to puke. But he took off his shirt—guys always have like two or three shirts on anyway—and allowed her to wrap her hand in it. Who could drive to the hospital? Oddly, me. So we went. We took the girl to the hospital, but it was late, and we said we couldn't stay and then we left, I guess, because we can be assholes sometimes.

Let me tell you something about blood. It's not a big deal for me. I watch as it drips into the sink and feel the same as I did two minutes ago before it happened. My thoughts of dying are no more or no less than usual. I am not going to faint. It's the tip of a finger, not an artery. But the longer I hold my hand over the sink, the longer no one else comes in to notice I need help, the more pink that chunk of cream cheese on the knife becomes, I feel panicky. It's startling, really, to see the inside of your body on the outside, to understand that one false move–one, tiny, unintentional missed step–makes such a mess.

I'm watching my heart beat. My heart is doing the job hearts are supposed to do, which is keep me alive, and I go around chopping myself to pieces. I think: pressure. Need pressure. The cut isn't that deep. I do my best to clean the cut with the hand soap on the edge of the sink, then open the first aid kit and take four band-aids out. Two for now, two for later.

Holding my injured hand up and away, I run water in the sink to wash away the blood, clean the knife really well and then use some Comet I find under the sink to scrub everything down.

I see Marie in her office looking at me the way my stepdad used to look at me, like my inaction and inability to notice tasks that need completing means I'm a failed human being. She motions for me to come in.

I sit in front of Marie and fold my hands in my lap. She's typing on her computer. Her short black hair tucked behind her ears. She lowers her glasses and looks at me.

"Shannon," she says.

"Yes," I respond.

"I'm making sure you are ok."

There's a picture of her and her husband on the desk. They volunteer. She never stops talking about it. Food banks. Animal shelters.

"I'm fine. Why?"

I am holding my injured finger away from my body.

She shuffles around some papers and extracts one, holds it in front of her. "You called in sick last week. You were late Monday."

I do not like to work in this office. "I'm sorry. I am. I've been busy with school, My car just took a—just needed to get some work done on it. Actually, I wondered if I could get some extra hours the next few weeks."

She leans over her desk at my bandaged hand but doesn't ask about it. "You want extra hours?"

"I can come in the mornings," I say.

Rebecca drove me to campus this morning then I walked here. My mother will have her car. So that'll work out. She can drive me here in the mornings while she goes around and looks for work.

Marie looks out beyond me and shakes her head at something or someone. She sighs. "All right. We can try it out. You know Bette is retiring soon, so we will need extra help."

A whisper of joy dances through me. Not because of Marie. My mom is coming. She really is.

"Great," I say. "Actually, it's my birthday."

I wait for her to say happy birthday but she doesn't. Anyway.

"My mom is coming up tonight. Uh, actually she's moving here. I wanted to know if I could take off a little early to get ready for her."

Marie sighs. Waves her hand. She's done with me.

I return to my desk. My inbox in my cubicle is overflowing, probably because I've been ignoring it. Everything lately is so needy. The only thing I've tacked up in my cubicle is a calendar the company handed out for Christmas. The Sonoran desert. This month, it's a Saguaro cactus at moonlight. Since I only come a few days during the week, sometimes when I arrive I get to cross more than one day off the calendar.

Taking my big black marker, I lean on the partition and x, x, x, which makes Bette, who sits on the other side say, "Is there an earthquake?"

She thinks she's funny, but it's passive-aggressive.

"I'm sorry," I say, not feeling sorry.

Bette answers phones because all the women here answer phones. The men here sell insurance. The older ladies in the back office forward emails warning me about men in parking lots offering perfume samples and men who attach themselves to the bottom of cars and slash the Achilles tendons of their victims before raping them and stealing all their money. After they eat their lunch sandwiches they sit at their desk with their little lipstick holders open, apply their colors, take a tissue, and blot. I hear Carmen's voice. She's chatting with one of the guys, but enters the breakroom alone. After filling her water bottle, and without looking at anyone, she walks out again. Carmen might be anorexic. I've never seen her eat.

Favoring my finger, I pick up the stack and go into the back room to file—the filing cabinet graveyard, I like to call it because the company hasn't replaced any of them in many years and the ones that aren't dented look like someone keyed them—determined to get the papers in those cabinets by five.

I slip a piece a paper into the C folder. What are other people doing right now to get by? Waitressing? Is that more fulfilling than singing the alphabet song in your head?

The day goes by fast, and before long, Rebecca is here, picking me up. She drops me at the apartment then takes off again, doesn't tell me what she's up to. I remind her my mother will be here when she gets back tonight. I rush into the house, excited and nervous.

When I go into my apartment, there's two messages. One from the garage. Guy telling me I absolutely need to pick up my car this week or else. I go into my bathroom to freshen up, i.e., reapply the lipstick I took from Rebecca's bathroom to cover the bruises on my lips and mouth.

A knock on my apartment door exactly at 4:30. My heart swells. I look out the peephole. My mother. As I watch, she glances behind her. Habit. My stepfather is never not on top of her, monitoring her every move. That'll take some time to get over. She wears a light, silk flowery scarf wrapped around her neck, a scarf that feels like a celebration. The scarf is more spring than winter, but she lives in the valley, forgets about weather in other places. Her coat is barely a coat, but I have an extra one for her. Or we could we go shopping. Coffee and shopping. After the bullshit of the last few weeks up here, seeing my mom on my doorstep makes me smile in a real way. I open the door all the way, ready to show her my place—our place until she gets on her feet, and I'm smiling so crazy it makes my lips hurt but I don't even care because she's here, finally she's here, and my stepfather is—he's—right behind her, puts his hand on her shoulder. My mother opens her mouth to speak, but he interrupts her.

"Hello Shannon," he says.

CHAPTER 10

My mother reaches out to touch my cheek but pulls back. "Happy birthday!"

I'm stunned. Voiceless. Nothing exists in me anymore. I look from her to Bill and back to her, and I see it in her face, in her eyes, that she's trying to explain it to me, she's trying to say she's sorry but what comes out of her mouth—

"Bill said he didn't want to miss your birthday," she says in her high-pitched Bill voice. She raises her eyebrows then, tilts her head slightly. Her signal to me that it's better to play along.

Feeling like I'm having an out-of-body experience, I reach forward to hug her. She's lost weight since Christmas. If that's even possible. When she releases me, I turn to Bill and hug him as well.

"Thank you for coming," I say, my voice sounding foreign to me.

"Yeah," he says. "I'm hungry. Let's go."

My mother smiles, indicates I need to follow them, that same pleading look on her face. I grab my coat and purse and follow her out to their Buick, open the back door, brush the ashes off the seat, then get in.

Bill lights a cigarette, cracks his window. My mother in the front seat chatters on without turning around to face me.

"It's been a long drive," she says. "Bill wants to go to Olive Garden. Is that—so that's where we're going. Olive Garden is delicious, isn't it? Bill loves the Olive Garden." She puts her hand on his leg and leaves it there.

I turn my head, watch the town go by. It's cold, but the sun is out so people are out. We pass downtown. The crystal shop. The one my mom wanted to go into last time they were here, but my stepfather said no. She doesn't say anything as we pass by. My stepdad ashes, and some of the ash flies back and lands on me.

"Oh, and there's your school," my mother says as we pass Benton State. "Isn't that your old dorm?"

My stepdad is silent. I don't answer. My mom stops talking. The dread my stepdad brings along with him settles into me. I try to rub the ash off my coat, but it leaves a black mark.

*

The Olive Garden hostess—clad in all black—leads us through the restaurant and toward the back, where we're seated in a booth off to the left away from the windows. My stepdad gestures for my mom to get in first, so she scoots over hefting her purse in front of her and then sticking it in the corner next to her.

The hostess passes around menus. My stepdad holds out his hand to my mom, who retrieves his black rimmed reading glasses from her purse as he browses the menu.

A waiter approaches the table. He is faux-fancy like this whole place. He wears black pants and a white button-down shirt tucked in. He tells us his name is Mark. Mark is tall and he has blonde-ish hair that's shaved close to his head like he's left the military but can't make the full adjustment. He asks how we're all doing. He says he's glad to hear it.

My stepdad asks for three waters, a beer for himself, and two glasses of house red for my mom and me.

"Oh, no thank you," I say.

"Shannon! It's your birthday! Let Bill get you a drink!" my mom says. "It's her 21st birthday."

"Really, I'm fine. I'm good with water," I say.

"Are you sick, girl? You never turn down a drink," my stepdad says.

Forgetting myself, I speak up. I hold up my hand. "Honestly, I don't want any wine. No thank you."

"We're offering you a drink," my stepdad says, his voice rising enough to that place I know and understand.

Mark needs to see my ID. I show him. He scans it. Passes it back to me with a smile. I don't smile back. I hate wine. Hate. And I hate sitting across from my stepfather. And I hate my mother's hand on him. And I hate him.

Bill stretches then, grimaces, puts his hand on his lower back. My mother leans in, says something I can't hear. I sip my water, glance around the restaurant, which is only half full.

"Poor Bill has to drive so much during the week. His back is bothering him," she says and pats his shoulder.

"You could have split the driving," I say without thinking. "If you can stand my mom's driving."

My stepfather laughs, and this was my intention. He is diffused. He likes people to take his side. You learn quick what you need to do to get through a day with him.

My stepdad has stretched one arm across the back of the booth and the other rests on the table. He's looking up at a painting above us. The painting is a bowl of grapes.

I can see my mom deflate for a moment and then pick herself up. She puts her hand on my stepdad's shoulder. He continues to gaze up at the grapes. She smiles at him like she's waiting for him to say something. She pats his chest.

"So, speaking of driving," I say and my mother clears her throat, traces lines on her water glass when I turn to her. She wants me to stop. "My car," I begin again but now she taps her fingers against the glass. Her signal to me that she thinks it's something Bill would get upset about, so she doesn't want me to go further, but I'm sort of hoping they'll offer to pay for some of it. Sometimes he does that. Throws down with money toward something. He pays for new clothes sometimes. He gives me gas money every so often.

"I'll tell you what happened. You bought a piece of shit car you had no business buying. You didn't think." He taps his forehead for emphasis. "What did I tell you when you went off to school? I said you didn't need a car. You could get around without one. Once you got out of school and got working, you could buy a nice car. You could afford it. But what did you do? You did what Shannon wanted to do, which was the wrong thing."

The drinks arrive, and now I do think a little hit of wine might feel nice. I wrap my hands around the stem of the glass. My mother's head is bent over the menu as though she's deep in thought about pasta. She slow taps her fingers, 1-2-3, on the table. She still wants me to drop it.

Bill takes a long drink of his beer. He's getting revved up, I can see it. Now, to divert.

"You're right, I know. I know," I say. "What are you getting, Mom?"

My mom waves her hand. "I don't even need to look at the menu. I'm getting the cheese ravioli. I've been looking forward to the cheese ravioli for weeks."

This Mark person, who's, like, standing in front of us, an absolutely abysmal portrait of a family, asks if we're ready to order. My mom and I, at the same time, look to my stepdad. Habits. All the habits. He nods to me. Permission to go first. I order a big bowl of pasta. Carbs, carbs, carbs. Mark asks my mother next, but my stepdad cuts her off and says the two of them will share the endless breadsticks and salad and the lasagna. He picks up my mom's menu and hands it back to the server. My mom doesn't skip a beat. She keeps smiling. She sips her drink and smiles and smiles and smiles.

The goddamn breadsticks show up, and I wait and my mother waits for my stepfather to take one. He then pushes the basket toward me, so I take one, break it in half and chew. My mother stares at the basket, then smiles at my stepfather, then says no thank you. I finish mine quickly and go for a second.

"Bread makes you fat," he says as I'm about to take a bite from the second one.

I take a bite anyway, then wipe the greasy Olive Garden bread butter on the cloth napkin. So consumed am I with my stepfather sitting at this table when I thought my mother and I would be having a celebratory glass of champagne tonight that I forget myself and wipe my mouth, the red lipstick coming off on the napkin. I stare down at the blood red stain then look up, my mother watching me. The bruising is exposed, and I let it sit in front of us, thinking she must, she will, see it this time. Mark the non-hero returns and places the salad between my stepfather and mother and me.

"Fresh parmesan?" he asks.

But my mother stares at me. She sees. I know she does. This is the reveal. My heart pounds. Emotion swells into a lump in my throat where it needs release. But it will not get any.

"Do you need anything else?" Mark asks.

My stepdad grins and says he needs a few thousand dollars. They both laugh—Mark for his tip and my stepdad for his dumb fucking joke every single man in this world makes. My mother directs her attention to my stepfather and joins the laughter. I put my elbow on the table and put my fist over my mouth.

My ice water glass sweats.

"Happy birthday, Shannon," my mom said and slides a red card across the table to me. My name in my mom's handwriting across the front. She glances at my stepdad and then nods to me. "Go ahead and open it."

I open the card. My hands are shaking. I smile and try to open it faster. The card has a picture of two stick-figured women drinking wine at a high-top table and chairs. The women's hair is wild.

Inside it says: Cheers to my most favorite girlfriend!

My mom has written, "Happy birthday Shannon! We love you!"

There is a gift card to Starbucks for $20. I close up the card and put it in my purse.

"Thank you so much," I say.

"You're welcome."

I excuse myself to the bathroom where I reapply my lipstick, and when I return, my stepfather is well into the lasagna. My mother's fork is in the air, hovering over him, waiting for an in. My pasta is in front of me, but I don't even want it. I twirl pasta around my fork then open my mouth to eat it, but don't know how I'll pull that off without wrecking the lipstick.

My mom clears her throat. Bill nods to her. "You know, Bill actually surprised me with a trip to Laughlin." She takes her napkin off her lap and places it on the table. "So we're going there from here."

I push my food around as my stepfather finishes most of their plate, and before long, Mark is back with a dessert. Jesus Christ. He's about to clap and dance and perform the fuckery Olive Garden calls a happy birthday song. I raise my hand. This is unnecessary. No singing or dancing for me, thanks. My stepfather pushes his dishes to the edge of the table. My mother delicately wipes her mouth and folds her napkin on the table. He puts the Double Fudge Extreme on the table. Two brownies with a scoop of ice-cream. Whipped cream on top. He sets in the middle of the table then gives us three spoons.

"This is compliments from Kevin," Mark says, and I whip around.

Wait, what? Who? *What?*

"He said to put extra whip on for you, and he said to say happy birthday again."

My mom's face is all lit up. Like this is the most excited I've seen her since she arrived. I quick look around the restaurant. Is he here? Did he follow me?

"Who's Kevin?" she asks. She picks up her fork and scoops some brownie onto it and eats it, then freezes, realizes my stepfather hasn't started to eat yet. He's staring at me, seemingly not concerned with her at the moment.

"He works here," Mark says. "He's over there."

Kevin, who had been watching, ducks behind a plant.

"Kevin is no one," I say and reach forward for a fork.

My mom takes my wrist, examines the bracelet.
"That's beautiful, honey. Is that from Kevin?"

"He's not no one," my stepdad says. "He bought you dessert. You must be doing something for him."

I remove some of the whipped cream from the top and put it in a napkin and stab a small piece of brownie.

"This is probably the best brownie I've ever had," she says.

I eat a piece of the brownie and chew it. It tastes like nothing—like a hard, bland nothing. I chew. And chew. It's dissolving in my mouth. I can't make myself swallow, like suddenly I don't know how to swallow anymore. Mmmm, my mom says again. She's eaten half the dessert. My stepdad has picked up his own fork. He's not even trying to manage her meal. The two of them dig into it like they've never eaten before in their lives. Meanwhile, I can't swallow. I cough. I pick up my water and force it down.

Mark has brought the check. My stepfather opens the billfold and stares into it for a long time while my mother and I sit in silence. I try to catch her eye but she is scraping the whipped cream off the plate.

"Thank you so much, Bill," she says and raises her eyebrow to me.

Bill glances off to the side as if he's bothered by our very existence. "Yep," he says.

"Thank you, Bill," I say.

He coughs his sick, pneumonia-like cough. Emphysema. My mother used to claim, perhaps may still claim, that he will die soon. When I was younger, I believed her. All we needed to do was wait him out. One morning, we'd wake up, and he'd be dead and we'd be free. I used to soothe myself to sleep at night by imagining him drowning in his own lung garbage. One morning he'd cough up so much shit he wouldn't be able to swallow, and he'd choke to death, collapse on the floor, writhing, and he'd look at me for help and I'd stand over him with the phone in my hand and then I'd ask

91

him how many crumbs under the microwave can he beat me for now and I'd laugh until he'd finished gasping and died.

"I'm so excited for our resort stay," my mom says. She smiles. "With Bill's schedule, we don't get much time together." My mom looks to my stepdad. "Two nights? Yes. Two nights."

Mark returns with the billfold. Three mints are inside. Bill passes one to me, one to my mom. He signs the paper then stands up.

"Let's go."

Bill stands and lets my mother out. Kevin is upon us then. A predator stalking a watering hole. My stepfather is a step or two ahead.

"Did you like the dessert?" he asks.

"I thought you were a hotshot."

"I am. Season starts soon. I work here in the off time."

I walk a little faster than him. My mother notices I'm not next to her, so she stops, sees Kevin.

"I'm June, Shannon's mother," she says and extends her hand.

A bold move since my stepfather doesn't like her interacting with the public.

"Thank you so much for that dessert," she says. "Delicious."

"Great, let's go, Mom," I say. For the first time maybe in my life, I'm grateful my stepfather is a controlling asshole. "Bill is waiting."

Bill is outside with a cigarette. When we walk out, he walks toward the car. I slow down, and my mom slows with me. Quietly I say, "I thought you were coming alone."

Anxious, her eyes dart around, place Bill out of earshot as he's already in the car. Quickly she says, "It wasn't the right time. But soon," and she gets in the car.

My stepfather lights another cigarette off the last one and smokes it to the end. We stop at a light and he rolls his window down, flicks it out, where I watch it land in the street, still smoldering. They let me out at my apartment. My mother doesn't get out to hug me. I tell them to have a nice trip.

My apartment is dark. Rebecca not home. I sit on the couch trying to process what I've been through the last two hours. Reflexively, I reach for the phone and call Daniel, who I haven't talked to since the weekend, and who, probably, I should say sorry to but, also, sometimes he really does talk too much.

When he answers, a simple and normal, "Hello," I find I cannot speak. "Hello?"

I'm sobbing.

"Shannon?"

I nod but of course he can't see that.

"Are you ok?"

I shake my head no, still heaving.

"Is it Andy?"

I shake my head no.

"Oh. Your mom."

Yes.

"All right. Take a breath. Take a deep breath. Do it with me. One, two, three. Breathe in and let go."

I do this.

"Again."

I do it again.

"Is that better?"

"Yes," I whisper. "She…"

"I know. I know," he says.

"No one loves me."

"Lots of people love you."

He's silent. I stand up and find tissue, blow my nose.

"I love you, all right?" he says. "I do. I love you."

A long, dark silence.

"You know, I love you…like…a friend. Like you're my friend," he says.

"I know. I'm sorry, Daniel."

"I know you are."

"I'm sorry. Will you stay on the phone with me until I fall asleep?" I ask.

I go into my room, pull the covers up over me and stay there. "Tell me a story," I say.

So he does. It's about Hadley's being overrun with well-read vampires.

CHAPTER 11

My phone rings at 6 a.m. It's my mother.

"Shannon," she says in her own, normal voice.

I sit up in bed. "What's wrong?"

"Bill and I had a fight," she says.

"Where are you?" I ask.

"I'm downstairs in the casino. I left the room. I just walked away from him," she says.

"You're in Laughlin? What does that mean, you walked away from him?"

"I left him. I walked out of the room."

I get out of bed and pace my bedroom.

"I mean, what's happening here? You're leaving him right now?" The sun isn't even up yet. "Do you need a ride? Do you want me to come get you?"

And how will I do that? I wipe junk out of my eyes.

"I'm looking into options," she says.

What did that even mean? I shake my head. Logistics later.

"Are you okay though?" I ask.

"I'm good, really. I feel very good right now. I feel amazing."

"You sound good!"

"I know!"

"I'll get a cab," she says. "I'm sorry. I am so sorry. At the last minute, maybe he sensed something, but he wanted to come with me. I couldn't stop him. I'm so sorry."

"It's ok. It's ok, Mom. Why don't you let me come get you?" I beg. "Which casino are you at?"

"Harrah's. Yes, that would be great. Come and get me, and then I'll come up to Benton and we'll do as we planned." She's quiet. "I see him walking around. He's looking for me. I'm going to disappear and wait for you. So, I'm in a pay phone near the front desk. There's a set of restrooms right here. I'll meet you in the restrooms. He can't come in to the women's restroom. All right? A few hours?"

"I'm coming." I say.

The line goes dead.

"Mom," I say into the phone but she's gone.

You always want to believe your parent. You always want to believe they are telling you the truth, and they have your best interest inside their heart. You need to believe they would never hurt you on purpose.

She is fine, I tell myself. She is fine. She'll lay low. I have a paper due today. It's half done but not all the way done. Rebecca shuffles out of her room, grabs a mug and waits. The biggest issue here, though, is I don't have a car.

"We're out of coffee cake," she says.

"I know."

A thought occurs to me. "What if we ditch class, get some real breakfast?"

"My dad doesn't put money in my account until the end of the week. I have like 14 dollars," she says. "Hey, let's go to Hadley's. Daniel will give us free food."

"I don't even know if Daniel is working."

She stops. Waits.

"What?"

"Are you and Daniel fighting?

"No."

"You don't ever not go to Hadley's."

"Yeah, and I eat a lot of their food and their food isn't healthy and maybe I want a break." I shake my head. "Let's do something different. Let's get out of town."

She crosses her arms. "What? I'm not leaving town." She walks past me and goes into her bedroom. "We have class this afternoon."

"I didn't finish my paper. I need to ask for an extension anyway. I'll tell her I'm sick. Or I have a family emergency."

That part isn't wrong.

"I have lab. I have notes to turn in."

"Say you're sick."

"I don't look sick."

"Don't you want to get out of town? It's nice out. Nice day for a drive."

"Don't *you* have Daniel to go do this stuff with? Daniel would drop his whole life if you called him to drive out of town." She raises her eyebrow. "Which further confirms you're fighting with him. Or you're busy fucking that other guy, and he's butt hurt about it."

"Well. Daniel is working. And we don't fight. I think it would be fun." I think fast. What would get Rebecca out of town? "Hey, um, let's go to Laughlin."

"Laughlin!" she laughs. "You're out of your mind."

"Why? Oh my gosh. It would be so fun." She's not buying it. "And, you know, there's that karaoke contest at, um, at Harrah's. It happens every Thursday."

This gets her.

"It's on the radio all the time," I say. "There's a cash prize. $500. You just said you don't have any money. You know you'd win." I see her turning it over. "I just got paid. I'll pay for your gas. And I'll buy lunch." I play my final card. "Is Gary home? He can come with us. He should come with us anyway to hear you sing."

She perks up. "Fuck it. Let's do it." She skips off to get Gary.

*

I go back to my room and brush my hair and put on more make-up. Rebecca comes back in the apartment with Gary trailing behind her. His hair is messy. I don't remember what Gary does for a living or why he would be home on a weekday.

"We're going to take Gary's car," she says. "It's newer. You got the MapQuest?"

I hold up the pages. Gary drives a brand-new white Toyota Corolla. You wouldn't think that by looking at him. You'd think he drove a douche faux sports car. I get in the backseat.

Rebecca claps her hands. "Ok, I'm excited now. This is fun."

Gary looks at me in the rearview. He puts his arm around Rebecca's headrest as he backs out. I hand him the directions. Tell him it's pretty much the 40 all the way.

We pass Mulligan's and Rebecca squeals. She turns to Gary. "That was my first karaoke contest. I won $50."

Hadley's is up ahead.

Under the Hadley's sign, it says, "Thank you Benton for 56 wonderful years!"

Like it's a marriage ending.

The university, the Olive Garden, Fillies, all of it ends up behind us. Gary pulls off into a Circle K before he merges onto the I-40. He lifts his hand off his steering wheel. He holds his hand back to me. Sign says gas is $1.23. I reach into my wallet, give him a 10.

The veil of daylight over the entrance of the store makes it look almost inviting. We open the door to all the colors—the back rows of red, blue, green sports drinks behind the coolers, the rows of candy, the advertisements for cigarettes. The clerk is a middle-aged woman with bleached hair and dark roots. She's sitting behind the counter looking down at her lap. She doesn't say hello to us.

Rebecca loads up a hot dog. I put my hand over the coffee pots. Warm. Working. She holds her hot dog out to me. "Do you want one?"

"Do I want a gas station hot dog?" I mean, I'm not against that but I feel a little sick from all the stress.

The guy in the trucker hat is in the store now, at the counter. He asks for a pack of cigarettes and a lottery ticket.

"I know. But these aren't bad," she says. She pumps ketchup.

Rebecca puts her back against the door, gives it a good shove so I can get through before it closes shut. We walk back to the car.

Rebecca slides her hand onto Gary's lap. "I'm kind of nervous," she says.

"I mean, it's an all new scene. I don't know what the atmosphere is going to be like. Kind of exciting though." She glances at me. "Why do you keep looking behind you? You're so jittery lately."

"I'm not looking behind me."

"You are. You're obsessing over someone."

Rebecca had been messing around with the radio before popping in a CD. Mariah Carey. She starts to sing. Harmonize. Do vocal warm-ups in the car on the highway. And I am borderline unclear if Rebecca thinks she sounds like Mariah Carey or? She's a good singer. A very good singer. But she's not Mariah *Carey*. I think about what I'll say to her when she finds out there is no karaoke contest. We pass the turn off to Daniel's place, and I hold my breath like I'm passing a cemetery. I watch the outside for awhile, the shadow of Gary's car jumping over other cars.

"By the way," she says, "I've barely talked to you, but, like, did you hook up with that hotshot?"

"Who's the hotshot?" Gary asks.

Christ.

"That guy she met at Fillies."

Gary shakes his head. He doesn't remember. "I don't remember."

Rebecca pats his arm. "Shannon's new love interest."

"Oh my god, he is not my new love interest."

"He's Shannon's new notch on the bedpost."

"Rebecca. No, he's not."

"I thought you said you slept with him."

"I never said that."

"Didn't you?"

"Not really."

We pass Love's, which is laden with semi-trucks. The car sways with each turn, and my body sways with it. Rebecca edges back toward me because she loves gossip.

"You did or you didn't."

"Let me ask you a question," I say.

"Shoot."

Shoot. I've heard Gary say shoot. Aggravating. Rebecca tends to pick up the language of her current sexual interest.

"Let's say you're with a guy, and you're not super sure you're going to sleep with him but then it happens," I say.

Rebecca looks at me like I'm dumb.

"Like, he just does it."

She fully shifts so she can look at me.

"Not like angrily or he's mad, he just kind of does it."

She taps Gary on the shoulder. He keeps his eyes on the road but turns his head toward her a second. "Listen to this," she says to him. To me, she says, "Say that again and ask Gary."

"I think Gary should focus on driving," I say.

Gary turns his head back. We're taking the short way around, the switchbacks that will then dump us out onto the 40.

"Like, you're making out and whatever and then he just says 'let's have sex' only he doesn't say that, he just does it."

No one responds.

"He just does it, like, has sex with you."

Rebecca keeps looking at me like she's not certain I'm done speaking. Around, around and down, down. My ears pop as we lower in elevation. My empty stomach less and less interested in absorbing the shock of the movement. The dizziness intensifies. Push it back. I take a small sip of water.

"I guess what I'm saying is I'm not sure if I have to count that kind of thing as a sexual encounter. Like, in the future, do I have to say, 'I've slept with two guys' when in fact

I've only really slept with one but the second was a weird thing?"

"I don't know if you have to count it. Maybe? Right?" She looks to Gary.

"Was there penetration?" Gary asks.

"Yeah."

"Then yes, you have to count it."

Rebecca opens a granola bar. She rips the top open, peels back the plastic and takes a bite. She swallows. "Probably. I think you have to count it."

"Penetration means it counts," Gary repeats.

My mouth waters but like how it does when you feel like you're going to throw up.

"Can I open a window?" I ask.

"Oh shit, are you going to throw up?" Rebecca asks. "Do you get car sick?"

"I'm fine," I say. I open the window and stick my nose against the fresh air. "I just need to breathe."

"I think Gary is right, actually. I think if you had full on sex with him, you have to count it." She takes another bite of granola bar.

"But it wasn't full on sex." Wait. "I guess it was, but it was just—weird. It was weird."

"Weird sex is still sex," Gary says.

I crank the window down a bit more and am blasted with wind.

"But what makes it sex? What makes sex, sex?"

"Penetration," Gary repeats.

"With a penis?"

"What else?"

"A million things. A million things can penetrate," Rebecca says. "So, wait. It was weird or it was bad?"

If I continue to talk, I will throw up all over this car.

"Holy shit—this is like seriously the best song," Rebecca turns back and turns up the volume. *Dreamlover* by Mariah Carey.

Gary puts the visor flap down to block the sun. I sit back and close my eyes for a second and that's a huge fucking mistake because the decentering makes me spin faster.

"Can we just stop for a minute? I just need to stop moving," I say.

"Here," Rebecca says. "Eat something." She tosses me a granola bar.

It's a Chewy, which is like eating air and chocolate chips. "I think I still need to stop."

"Don't throw up in my car," Gary says.

"Pull over and I won't," I say.

He parks on the side of the road, and I rush out of the car, make it into the brush and lean over. Nothing comes. I take a deep breath. Do not throw up. I sit on the ground in the dirt and rock. The ground is cold. I close my eyes and try to focus on breathing. Focus on replacing the polluted air from inside with better air. I breathe. I can see my breath in the air. Everything here is so still. I breathe. And breathe. And try to get all the still in me.

"Shannon?" Rebecca calls for me.

I don't answer. Something catches my eye just beyond the bushes. I stand, brush myself off and try to get a closer look.

"Shannon?" she calls again.

Movement. I freeze. It moves more, but doesn't progress, just kind of moves in place like a marching band keeping time. Then I see it's a dead bird. A large dead bird. Birds fly. Birds don't die on the road.

Something could have carried it here. Or maybe it fell out of the sky. It's moving because it is being consumed by maggots. I lose it then. Vomit it all up.

CHAPTER 12

Gary pulls up in front of Harrah's. We leave our coats in the car, including the one I brought for my mom. Rebecca and I go inside as Gary parks. And it's not until we arrive at this place, see the outside, see the place where I imagined she called me from, see the glitter and shine in the lobby that the relief sets in.

"Wait up," Rebecca calls out after me.

The directional signs say the lounge is to the left and registration is the right.

"I need to find the lounge and get signed up," Rebecca says.

"Yeah, yeah. Go on. I'll catch up."

I see the payphone she must have called from and go to it. Empty. I see the bathroom. I go inside. Empty.

"Mom?" I say, my voice echoes. I bend down, see if anyone is under the stalls. "Mom?"

No one is here. Which. Yes. She's not sitting in a bathroom for the day. She maybe got hungry. She might come back any second. The casino floor is a light show: pink and blue and green and yellow. Dinging and beeping and happy, musical sounds encapsulate each person sitting in front of a machine. I'm surrounded by quarter slots. My mom sometimes plays the quarter slots. She's more likely to play the quarter slots than the dollars. My stepdad likes to play the pennies. A woman in a gold body suit and a black, sequined vest in the highest of heels walks past with a tray of drinks. I smile at her. She wears bright red lipstick. Her dark hair is teased up and she's painted her eyes in dark green and black. We catch eyes but she doesn't smile or acknowledge me. I take my smile back.

A large woman in a pink dress and an oxygen tank gets up from the machine she'd been playing, a Wheel of Fortune game, but when she sees me approach, she sits back down and reinserts her player's card. An older man in a short-sleeved dress shirt and brown pants that are an inch too short for him has one hand against the machine like he's using it to hold himself up and he's using his other hand to press the button, press the button, press the button with this sad intensity like he knows—he knows—the next push is going to win, and it doesn't matter how many losses he rakes up because the next one will win, he knows this more than he knows anything else in his life, he will walk out of this casino with a win, he will win, he is a winner. The gold body suit cruises past and gives the middle-aged woman sitting two slots down from the man with the too short pants a brown, iced drink. The woman takes the drink and sips it before setting it down. She gives the gold body suit a dollar. The too short pants man flags her down and reshuffles his obsessive gaze, and she leans in to hear what he's saying, she nods, and she starts to walk away, but he calls her back, and she leans in again, and then she nods again, and he seems to call her back again but this time she gets away.

Fruit Mania. Malibu Madness. Glittering Retro Reels. Triple Shots. The poker machines. My stepdad would have played the poker machines. I keep walking.

Between the quarter slots and the penny slots is a red Chevy Malibu sectioned off with maroon velvet ropes. A woman rips off a sheet of paper and stuffs it in a clear, locked box next to the car. I linger a second around the box. Some of the papers are open and exposed. Russell Miller. Carolyn Miller. Maureen Begay. I know my mom hates that Buick my stepfather drives. We had a black Mazda for a long time, and my mom would always look at beige cars and say, "That's the color of car you buy when you're old." Beige is for when you give up.

I stand on my tiptoes and try to see inside the Chevy. Looks like tan interior. My mom probably stopped here and looked at the car, too. The clear box is stuffed. I tap the box, see if I can reshuffle the papers. Nothing moves. I shake the box but another gold body suit comes by and this one looks alive, looks right at me, so I write my name on the sheet and stuff in the box. I'm not against a brand new car.

The signs above me say the hotel lobby is ahead. I walk toward it, am still walking toward it when I see her and my shoulders relax and my heart stops racing.

"Mom?" I walk faster. The woman walks ahead of me. I walk even faster. "Mom?"

She turns then to reveal a high-tipped nose and bird-like lips. She's not my mom. "Sorry," I say.

The reddish gold carpet gives way to cream-colored tile and tall columns and a light perfume smell. Two people stand behind the counter dressed like flight attendants in blue sweater vests and maroon ties. A gift shop is off to my left, so I browse the pencils, towels, toy slot machines, gum, magazines, stuffed animals, ugly dresses, and bedazzled purses. I turn the postcard rack around one time not really looking at any of it. My mom might have purchased postcards. Always a safe bet for an inexpensive souvenir. Photographs of the casino are predominant but plenty of photos of Laughlin at night and sunsets are scattered throughout. One of the people working behind the front desk walks off. I approach.

"Hello," I say.

He is young, and his thick, black hair is pulled back in a long braid. "Good afternoon, are you checking in?"

"I need to call my mom. I'm being lazy and not going up to her room. I need to tell her something. Could you call her for me? Is that possible?"

"What's her room number?" He shifts over to his computer.

I tap my toe on the floor.

"You know, I don't know. I think it's 200 something. Can you look it up? I just want to tell her where I am. Her name is June Walker."

Saying my mom's name makes her real here. She existed in this space. He taps away on his keyboard. I'd been leaning into the marble counter, and I pull my hands away leaving a sweaty trail.

"I'm not seeing a June Walker," he says.

"Of course, sorry, it's under my stepdad's name. Bill Walker. William."

"No," he says. "Oh. Yes. I do see a Bill Walker. He checked out this morning."

The ride I feel like I've been on slows to a stop, and the bars raise, and it's time to step out, but I'm disoriented from the rush.

"Were you here," I ask thickly. "Did he check out alone?"

"I'm sorry. I wasn't on yet."

"Oh my god," a voice behind me says.

I turn. Rebecca. Alone.

"Jesus. You scared me," I say.

"What are you doing?"

I put my hand over my heart. "Seriously. You like gave me a heart attack."

Front Desk's phone rings. He says excuse me. I move away from the desk, and she does the same.

"Is your mom here?" Rebecca asks. Her eyes widen and then narrow again as she figures out what happened. What might be happening. "Oh my god. Is that why we're here? Because it's not karaoke. Like no one knows what the fuck I'm talking about, and I look like an idiot."

"No," I say, panic still rising. This is probably not a lie. "My mom is not here."

Front desk hangs up the phone, and Rebecca turns back to him. She believes she's caught me, so she sidles up to the desk all smug and self-assured.

"Good afternoon, ma'am. Are you checking in?"

She props her arm on the counter. "Could you tell me what time the karaoke contest starts tonight?"

This must be what it feels like to die. I'm dying. My insides are eating itself. I clutch my stomach.

"Not tonight, miss."

"Ah," she says and crosses her arms. "No karaoke tonight, you say?"

"We have karaoke on Saturdays. Tonight is the drag show."

I throw my hands up. "I must have heard it wrong. Must have." I take her arm, lead her away. "Anyway, it's still a fun day. There's Gary. He parked the car like a nice man. Let's get a drink."

Emphasis on man. Seriously, how old is Gary? She puts her hand in his, and I'm alone again.

The penny slots area is more populated. A girl who looks my age sits in a red crop top and jeans, her belly hanging out and over. A gold body suit appears behind me—same one with the heavy make-up and asks if I'd like a drink. A man three machines down drinks a beer. He holds his beer to me.

"I'll have a rum and Coke," I say.

I open my purse. "Complimentary two drinks at the machines," she says.

"Oh. Right Great. Thank you."

She walks away. I light a cigarette with the half empty pack of matches next to the machine.

Man drinking a beer is a dad's age. I turn my body away from him. The signs above me point to the hotel lobby. My mom could have been sitting at this machine. She could have been idling here, pressing buttons, drinking free, cheap wine, enjoying a day off from her job talking to my stepdad about his fucking road stories.

The man walks toward me now just as the gold bodysuit brings me my drink. She hands it over. For her tip, I give her the dollar's worth of change and don't look her in the eye.

"Thanks," I say.

"What are you drinking?" The man stands above me.

"Rum and Coke," I say, looking up.

He sits at the machine next to me. Legs splayed. He wears a gold wedding band.

"I'll get you another one," he says.

"They're complimentary," I say.

"That's the swill. You have to buy the better drinks with the more expensive alcohol."

His hair is dark, save for the light spray painting of gray around his temples. You can tell when he was younger and had more weight on him, he was probably somewhat attractive. He looks down at his ring because that's where I'm looking. He thumbs the gold band. "My wife died last year."

"Oh," I say and fall off guard for a second. "I'm sorry to hear that."

He scoots toward me. "It's hard." He waves then for a gold body suit. One approaches. "Sweetheart, can you bring this young lady a *Bacardi* and Coke?"

I turn to her expecting to hear myself say no thanks. But I nod yes. He leans in to my machine. "You're out of money. Here," he says. His reaches for his wallet. Extracts a 10 dollar bill. Reaches past me and inserts it.

My mom says when she goes to the casino, she only plays with $20. She either doubles it or loses it, but once the $20 is gone she stops, so she'll do her best to stretch it.

The man pushes the max bet. "Always hit the max bet. It's your best chance to win." His cologne is old man cologne. His gray chest hair pokes out of his polo shirt. A line hits. "Cherries always win for me," he says. I get 300 points. I never win on these things. That's exciting, and I turn to him and smile before catching myself. His breath smells like beer. "I must be your lucky charm. Let's double down." He pushes max bet again, takes another drink of his beer. His body blocks my rum and Coke. I'd have to touch him to get to it. No lines hit this time. He pushes max bet yet again. No hit. The gold body suit returns. She gives my rum and Coke and another beer to the man. He gives her a $20 bill. He tells her to keep the change. She smiles at him.

"Thanks hon," she says.

Back on me. "Go ahead, try it. It's better with the brand stuff, trust me."

With him watching, I drink out of the straw. He sits sideways in the chair with his hand resting on the back of my chair.

"What do you think?"

That Chewy bar is long gone, so the alcohol falls on an empty stomach. The first one already went to my head. I honestly don't notice that much of a difference, but I'm afraid to tell him that.

"It's good."

"Drink it fast," he says, "the ice will melt. You don't want it watered down."

"Shannon?" A male voice calls my name.

The man straightens, moves his energy away from me, and I come back to myself. Gary approaches from behind. He does not acknowledge the man who has taken a full step back. Gary is taller than him. "Hello!" I say.

"Rebecca wanted me—"

I put my arm through his. "I was wondering where you went."

The man takes one more step back.

"We were—

"Let me finish my game, and then we'll go," I say.

I turn back to the machine. I hit max bet. Max bet. Max bet until all the money is gone. The man fully retreats.

"Thanks for saving me," I say to Gary.

For an odd flash, I get Gary's appeal. I get his size, his voice. For extra pizzaz, I slip my arm through his and he pulls me close to him. We walk out of the slots, pass back through the hotel lobby and the front desk. We walk together, in step, like we are together, like I belong to someone, like someone loves me enough to want to show me off. A middle-aged couple walks a beat ahead of us and stops at the desk. The man puts a bag down and the woman hefts her purse onto the counter.

Rebecca rushes toward us and stops. Gary slips his arm off me. "Come on," she says with a second glance back at me and a small frown. "The drag show is starting."

Rebecca leads us to a table near the front. Approximately ten other disenchanted people sit at tables behind us. The lounge is smoky. An ashtray is on the table, so I light a cigarette. Rebecca stares at the stage, enraptured. The black backdrop is decorated with stars. A single plant is on one side.

"I love drag shows," she says.

"When have you been to a drag show?"

"I went with my stepmom and stepsister last year," she says. "We had a blast."

"What was the deal with that guy?" Gary asks.

I look at him, almost surprised he's speaking to me. "The man at the machines? He was hitting on me."

I say this in a specific way. Gary, guys hit on me. I have something they want. Gary, I am desirable. A server first asks me and Rebecca for ID, then asks if we'd like drinks. Of course we'd like drinks.

The lights dim. A bright yellow spotlight hits the stage. "Ladies and Gentlemen," an announcer says, "the Queens would like to welcome you to Harrah's!"

Rebecca claps.

"We have a special guest tonight, all the way from New York on her way to the Drag Queen World Series taking place next month in Los Angeles, Ms. Chantel M. Riveria."

The opening riff to a remix of *Supermodel* blasts out. A figure emerges from behind the curtain. The music stops a split second and the lights go out. The lights and the music ignite again and a tall, blonde woman with legs that go for miles walks out on the stage in a brilliant white dress and bold, red lips.

She mouths along to the music. *You. Better. Work.* Then she snaps her fingers.

The music picks up and she sashays to the front of the stage. A few more people have entered the lounge. Rebecca hovers at the front of the stage and waves a dollar. Ms. Chantel accepts the money and blows Rebecca a kiss.

Ms. Chantal smiles like she has something on her teeth that tastes bad. Rebecca waves her over and offers her another dollar. This time, the woman takes Rebecca's hand and gives it a squeeze.

The song ends. The drinks arrive. I drink my rum and Coke very fast because I am thirsty. The ice melts. I light another cigarette. Gary sips his beer. The blonde woman leaves the stage, and the next one comes out, this woman shorter with a little more weight to her but more exotic-looking. Her hair is bright red. Rebecca claps for her. I've never seen her more excited. The bright redheaded woman saunters to Rebecca first. She's lip-syncing *I Will Survive*. Rebecca gives her money and sings as loud as the music.

A few more people from inside the casino have filled in. Rebecca is nearly on the stage giving the performers more dollars like we're at a strip club. It is unclear to me if this is what we're all supposed to be doing. "This is so fucking fun," she says to me. "Get up here." But then dances off again.

I order a grilled cheese and French fries from our server. My mom and I used to have grilled cheeses all the time. It's cheap and easy. For awhile, before she met my stepdad, the two of us just hung out in our motel room eating grilled cheese sandwiches watching 80s Brat Pack movies. She met my stepfather at her job. We were living in his house within three months.

The first and second women are back on stage together both performing a remix of Cher—1960s Cher and then 1980s Cher. My food arrives. The ketchup bottle is already on the table, so I squeeze a bit on the greasy paper inside the basket, careful not to get any on the sandwich. Gary takes a French fry, then another. He dips the second one in the ketchup.

Everything slows and becomes awful again. Gary takes another fry. I stand too fast and feel woozy, put my hands on the table to steady myself. "I'll be right back," I say.

On second thought, I swipe both halves of the sandwich. I leave the fries.

*

I take another bite of the sandwich and have to move out of the way for a group of laughing and hysterically alive people. The dinging machines surround me. The neon lights snap. A woman and man cut in front of me. They hold hands.

The grilled cheese crumbles in my hand. The outer edges just a second overdone. Bits of toast flake off. I wipe my hands on my jeans leaving grease streaks. See how I ruin everything.

The ATM sits alone in the corner. Poor ATM machine without friends or anyone who loves it. One-handed, I insert my card. Stupid fee. Fucking, stupid fee. $20. I look at my receipt. I have $18 in my checking account. Rebecca handily handing dollars to the queens. Handily handing. Haha. I shake my head and finish the first half of one sandwich and get through most of the second, but I still have the crust. No one likes the fucking crust. My mom always ate the crust I didn't eat. She'd watch me. Wait me out. Reach across the table like Renfield and snatch the crust and gobble it up.

I sit down at a poker machine and pick the standard poker game. I push the $20 in. Ante. The machine deals the cards. King, 4, 8, 2, Ace. I keep the King and the Ace. The machine comes back at me with 7, 8, 4. Game over.

The bathrooms are back by the lounge. I have to go to the bathroom. The World Series of Drag Queens stands at the mirror and applies lipstick. She pouts her lips, then smiles, then pouts again. Her eyelashes flirt with the mirror. She is more than six feet tall in those heels. I am small.

"Oh," I say. "Sorry." I feel like I've caught her in her dressing room.

She caps her lipstick. "It's a public restroom, honey," she says. Her great big eyelashes dip down, then up. "You're free to use it. Honey, are you looking for a trash can?"

The grilled cheese crust. I toss it in the almost overflowing paper towel trash bin.

She turns her full attention to me. Up close, her face is flawless. I can't even see the make-up line. I wish I could do make-up like that. She looks as though she soaks in lotion.

"You're beautiful," I say.

"Aw, thank you honey," she says. She reaches out to touch my face. "Beauty comes from believing in yourself." She then puts the back of her hand on my cheek, then feels my forehead. "Honey, you don't look good." Then she's gone. Whoosh.

I'm alone.

I feel woozy. Off. She's not wrong. My eyes are glassy but the bruises around my mouth are healing. I see then a small piece of paper with an S on the front. A short note written on hotel stationary.

Shannon – I'm ok! Bill and I talked. We decided to go home early. I'm so sorry again. I love you. Love, Mom.

I crumple the paper and hold it over the trash, ready to toss it but then stuff it in my pocket. I return to the lounge, open my purse for my cigarettes and birth control pills. I open the pack under the table. I swallow three pills in a row then light a cigarette.

Rebecca has made it to the first step of the stage, mimicking the queen's dancing and singing Madonna with them. She waves to me.

That old dirty man from earlier sits near us next to a woman who is his age if not older. She wears khakis. They swing. She removes her dark blue blazer and drapes it over the back of her chair.

The song ends, and Rebecca is the most fucking hyped person in the room. The server sets down a glass of water.

"This was the best time I've had in a long time," Rebecca says, drinking my water.

The lights come back.

"Hey, I'm ready to go when you guys are," I say.

Rebecca doesn't hear me. She gives Gary an impromptu lap dance sans music. I tap Gary on the arm. "Hey," I say. "Are you ready to go?"

"Ugh, you guys suck," says Rebecca as she removes her leg from around Gary. "Fine. Let's go."

She dances out of the casino, and Gary follows behind. I linger a moment in front of the stage. A band sets up. The woman with the man from the slots puts her hand on his back and pats him, and he turns to her and smiles, and she smiles back. They look happy. I walk to their table. I stand in front of them, the man looks up at me, recognizes me, sits up, and the woman remains relaxed, confused the longer I stand and stare at them. The woman's hair is not colored. Her gray is interspersed throughout. She wears unassuming gold hoops in each ear.

I address the man direct. "I'm very sorry."

She looks to the man and back to me.

"I'm very sorry again for your loss," I say to him.

Then I walk away. She'll ask what that was all about. The lie he tells her will be enough to keep their marriage going.

As we reach the exit doors, Gary veers and says he has to use the restroom. He reaches into his pocket and hands Rebecca his keys, says he's in row G. She makes sure he's out of range, and she dangles the keys in front of me and grins. We push through the doors.

"I've got his keys," she sings and shakes them like a rattle. "I've got his keys."

Rebecca thinks car keys are a sign of intimacy. She presses the button and Gary's car lights up. I open the back door and crawl in while Rebecca gets situated up front. Her door is still open. The car dings its displeasure.

"That's making me nuts," I say. "Shut the door."

"Hold on," she says. "I need the light for a second."

"I'm cold," I say.

"Hold *on*," she says.

Something glistens in the backseat. I pick it up. Rebecca turns back to say something to me as I hold it. A small object. Black and sparkling.

"What's that?"

My earring. I brought it. It's mine. "I don't know," I say.

"Give that to me," she says.

She takes the black rhinestone earring, holds it to the light. She looks confused. Her lower lip trembles for about a half second.

"Gary has a sister, right?" I ask.

She doesn't answer.

"Right?"

"This thing could have been in the car for like, months."

"It's Megan's," she says.

She crosses her arms. Gary opens the car door then and gets in. The car shifts with his weight.

"I thought the heat would be on," he says.

"I didn't know how to work your car," she says.

"Baby, it's just a car," he says. "It's like all the other cars." He reaches his hand out and Rebecca drops the keys in his palm.

Gary whistles as he starts the car. "Don't throw up on the way home," he says to me.

Rebecca stares ahead as Gary's hand creeps over but she slaps him away.

"What the fuck?" he says.

115

They argue for the entire drive home. Gary is a pig and a liar. Just because there's an earring in here doesn't mean anything, I gave her a ride once, and Rebecca practically screamed *I'll bet you did*, Gary calls her crazy and jealous and on and on and it's like they've forgotten I'm sitting back here. Poof. Where's Shannon? Shannon has been sucked up in into the ether.

When we finally get home, I can't get out of the car fast enough, I practically shoulder roll out while it's still in motion. Their voices behind me—maybe they'll end the night fucking or maybe they'll never speak to each other again—I rush over to the mail box. An unmarked envelope with my name on it. I feel the outside of it. Feels like a credit card. It IS a credit card. Oh, I am saved. I am so fucking saved. I tear the envelope open. Yes. Oh my god, yes. It's only a $3,000 limit, not the $3,500 but that is enough. I can get my car back. I press it to my chest. I can get my fucking car back. Inside the apartment, there's a message waiting for me. I press it, expecting to hear— I don't know—my mother saying she's sorry for every choice she's ever made since I was 11-years-old but it's Andy. Asking me to call him. I don't get through the whole message before I pick up the phone and call him. He answers on the second ring. A miracle!

"Hey," he says and his voice is like energy moving into my bloodstream, and I'm warm again, and this feeling spreads through my body. Peace. I am, for the first time in days, weeks, months, peaceful.

"Hey," I say back.

He's quiet.

"You called?"

"Oh. Yeah, some friends are getting married up there."

"Right. You mentioned that."

"Oh."

"Where are they getting married?"

He rustles around. Sounds like papers or a bong or I don't know. "Some place with a mill."

Doesn't matter.

"I wanted to know if you're around, if we can hang out."

"Of course," I say, and I almost start crying.

"I'll call you when I get there," he says.

"I—"

I almost said it. I miss you. Almost fucking said it.

"I'll talk to you then," I say.

"Right, see you," he says and the line goes dead.

Rebecca comes in the front door consumed with darkness, and I step into the living room holding the phone like I'm on it even though now I have the dial tone. She goes into her room, slams the door, and then I hear Hole's Celebrity Skin blasting out, and then I realize that is my CD.

CHAPTER 13

Most of my classes this semester are on North campus, the
older part of the university. I love these old buildings. They're
full of ghosts. My history professor's office is on the third floor
of Elm, so I trudge up the stairs and am winded by the time I
reach her office. Dr. Roberson is a middle-aged woman,
blonde, blunt-cut shoulder-length hair. She's always in a
sweater-set and black pants and pearls. We agreed for me to
come to her office so I could drop off my late paper.

My sunglasses are still on when I tap on her door even
though it's open. She has Far Side cartoons taped up outside
her office, and inside, she's surrounded by books and a neat,
organized desk. She looks up and smiles at me. Her violet
sweater-set is set against a pair of jeans today.

"Thank you, Shannon," she says as I hand her my
paper. "Is your future bright?"

"What?"

She taps her head. "Your sunglasses."

"Oh," I say and take them off. "Sorry."

She holds up her hand. "That's fine. You don't have to
explain yourself." She runs her eyes up and down my paper
and doesn't speak.

"All right, thanks again," I say and turn to leave.

"Hold on," she says.

"If you came to class and did your work on time, you
wouldn't have to take extra time to get your work in."

I stare at the floor. "Yeah. I know. I've had a lot of stuff
going on."

"In skimming this, I know this paper will be good.
You're a good writer. When you put effort into something, it
shows."

Jesus.

"I have to get to work," I say.

"Where do you work?"

I thumb behind me. "Insurance agency. Office help."

"Do you like it?"

"I don't know. Not really. It's boring."

"Do you want to work in insurance?"

I laugh. "No. I found the job through a job board, and they work around my class schedule."

"What do you want to do after school?" She laughs at herself then. "I'm sure I sound like your parents."

I bristle. "You don't."

Honestly, I do not believe my mother has asked me what I want to do after school. We have limited time in our conversations because of my stepfather, and most of the time when she is free to talk, we talk about how she needs to leave him.

"Ah," she says. She folds her hands across her stomach. "Shannon. I'm only saying this to you because, again, I very much enjoyed your first paper and think you show an abundance of potential. Most of my students who don't show up to class also don't write papers like you wrote." She seems to get distracted by her own thoughts. "What's your major?"

"Advertising. Tricking people for a living." I say and laugh but she doesn't. "I needed a humanities credit."

"We're about to post a job for an office assistant here. Filing, copying, things like that. Maybe potential for more."

She stands up, takes me down the quiet hall. We go into the main office, and she pulls a piece of paper off the printer.

I stare at it. It's just a job posting outlining crummy office duties I already hate. A few words toward the bottom catch my eye. Writing skills. Assistance with research projects.

"You let undergrads help with research projects?"

"The admin end of it, yes. Might involve making some phone calls or copying papers or document transfers but yes." She offers an almost motherly smile. "Think about it."

I slip the paper into my folder. "I will."

"We're a tight department here and I think you'd fit in. You're smart, Shannon."

I push my sunglasses on, turn to leave.

"I'll see you in class next week," she says. "And that's a great color lipstick on you."

I touch my mouth. "Thanks," I say.

Buoyed by this vague level of praise—you'd do better if you did better—I stop at the mall on my way home. It's Andy Day. I walk into Victoria's Secret. Vicky's Secret, Rebecca and I say. A sales girl approaches with a measuring tape. You want me to measure you? Measure you? Can I measure you? Do you need to be measured? Measured? Are you measured? Have you been measured.

No, no, no, I say and rush into the back holding a black lace bra and a purple lace bra and a baby blue bra, and the girl checking people into the dressing room has a measuring tape around her neck. I'll give you a room but *have you been measured?*

I take off my shirt and my bra—the only one I have left because I pitched that one I wore to see the hotshot. I turn from one side to the other. I put the black one on first and it's too small. I set it aside and try the purple. Small. Kill me. I have to be measured. I don't even know how that's possible. I put my clothes back on, tell the girl the bras didn't work out, but go onto the floor and just grab one cup size up. I'm eating garbage. Pizza. Chips. Coffee cake. It's going into my boobs, I guess. Maybe not a bad thing.

I buy two bras and matching panty sets, and then five pairs of under because it's 5 for $35, and the sales girl asks if I want to be in the Victoria's Secret club, yeah, sure, and she asks if I want to open a credit card and I say, yeah sure, and somehow or another I get preapproved so she rings me up, and I leave the store feeling good and positive, like no one is going to accuse me of having granny panties.

I pass Waldenbooks and remember Daniel's birthday in a few months. I should get him a gift card. I keep walking.

In Maurice's, I try on a bunch of clothes, but I don't know what I'm supposed to wear to a wedding. I settle on a black faux suede skirt and a gray fuzzy sweater.

I do the slow walk out through Dillard's and stand too long in front of the Clinique counter where an older woman asks what my skincare routine is, and I'm like, I don't have a skincare routine? You have to wash your face. Well, obviously. You have to exfoliate. Moisturize. You have to wear sunscreen.

I quote the song back to her. "I don't know much, but I know this: wear sunscreen."

Those are the wrong lyrics. She doesn't know what I'm talking about. Clearly you weren't graduating high school in 1997.

Anyway, she lines up products. Asks for my hand. Gets out a bowl. Washes the back of my hand in the bowl, moisturizes my hand, puts sunscreen on my hand. Feels nice. Smooth.

She tells me to sit. Puts my face under a light and mirror. Those lines, she says. Lines around your face. I touch my face like I've been slapped. We stop lines with sunscreen and moisturizer.

Then, I don't know why, I start telling her about my date. About Andy. He's tall. He has a great voice. Good hands. We met at the beach. He was riding a jet ski. She puts blush on my cheeks. Says "mmmmmm" a bunch of times then tells me the right way to put on mascara. Do I have an eyelash curler? Do I have blush brushes? Do I know what to do with my cheekbones?

My mom told me how hard it was being with my dad, but in the end, you know, she got him. And she got me. And here I am. And I don't know where my real father is. And that, my mother tells me, is for the best.

The woman shows me my face in the mirror. The make-up is nice. I look like me, only enhanced. She rings up my purchases. I give her my credit card. She says to have a nice time with my boyfriend. I take that inside and let it turn, slowly, and I feel a small boost. It feels nice to believe.

CHAPTER 14

I'm nervous, so I smoke a cigarette, dumb, because nicotine is
a stimulant but it's also an addiction and soothing the
addiction calms the body, at least for 10 minutes. I make myself
a drink. A shot of vodka in a half glass of orange while Rebecca
stalks around the apartment cursing and throwing things.
She's in black sweat pants and a gray hoodie, old mascara
smeared under her eyes. I set the bottle of vodka on the
counter then Rebecca swipes it up, pours herself a shot and
then yells out how she's surprised men haven't found a way to
marry their own dicks. She slams her bedroom door shut, and
it's Fiona Apple who seeps under the door. I peek out the
window. Gary's apartment is dark. Curtains closed.

I pull on the black nylons and the skirt and the sweater
and the shoes, and it's already 4 o'clock. I don't know what
time weddings start, but I feel like it should be soon. I sit on the
couch, smooth my skirt, and then I stand and pace and go
outside for another cigarette. A man walks by and coughs.

I turn on the TV. Local news. Weather. Cold and dry. I
stand up. Pace again. It's 4:30. I take off my shoes. They're not
comfortable. I go outside for another cigarette and when I
come back in, a man's voice is on the answering machine and I
rush for it, but it's Daniel, and I pull back like the phone is a
disease. Adrian borrowed his car. He's carless. Am I interested
in dinner? Do I want to pick him up for dinner? Do I want to
come get him? He hopes my car is good. Assumes it is since I
haven't said otherwise. Can I call him?

I pull the phonebook out from under the coffee table,
turn over to…what? Wedding venues. He said Mill. Is he
talking about the Old Mill? I call their number. No one
answers, but they do say they're a wedding venue, and if I'm
interested in having my wedding at Old Mill, I can leave my
information and someone will call me. A bizarre way of nausea
overtakes me, and I have to sit. Shake it off. Andy wants me to

go to this wedding with him, which means that he sees himself getting married, maybe even to me. Wedding invites are not lighthearted casual events.

Did he call, and I missed it?

Did he give me other instructions, and I missed them?

Is he out there waiting for me?

My drink is gone, and my cigarettes are half gone, and I turn on the computer and MapQuest the directions to Old Mill.

Old Mill is on the way to the ski resort. I smoke three cigarettes and listen to Natalie Imbruglia. Instead of throwing the butts out the window, I put them in an empty can of Diet Cherry Coke.

I drive up the main driveway until I hit a line of cars. This seems…wedding-ish. Yeah, definitely something going on here. I park. Check my face in the mirror. Tuck my hair back. Put on a little more lipstick. The light is longer now, but still, we're looking at sunset soon. I get out of the car and trudge up the rocky dirt road in my heels until I reach the main hall. There must be 200 people in here. I settle in with the smokers. Bum a smoke and a light from someone named Charlie, who is not at all cute. Like, he's not not cute but he's not cute. He's a Daniel. A teddy bear. Someone to cuddle with, cry on. He makes a joke about Kid Rock being greasy and everyone laughs, and I laugh, and I'm having a good time wondering if these are Andy's friends, and if they like me. I dip a toe in the water. Do you guys know Andy? Andy Cousins? Oh yeah, they all say. Andy is our buddy. He's up there. I thank them, especially Charlie, who offers to walk me up, but I say no thank you. Inside the hall, it's even more crowded and the DJ is playing Shout and everyone has their hands in the air. The bride is dancing with a group of bridesmaids who are all in long, lavender chiffon dresses.

The hall is all wood. Wood floor. Wood ceiling. Barnish without being a barn. White tablecloths. Spring flowers even though it isn't fully spring. Pretty.

Then I see him. Standing with another guy. Both of them holding longnecks. That warm Andy feeling comes over me.

We did meet on a beach. He was so hot, like prince of the lake level of hot. Shirtless. Tan. Broad-shouldered. 6'3". He dismounted and came for me. I can't even stand thinking about it. I'd never had a boyfriend. Had one date in high school, but it didn't count. My best guy friend took me to prom, and I watched my crush dance with his date all night. Andy was like, who are you, where are you from, why are you so beautiful and alone, and he drove me home after our first date to a movie and touched my hair and said he couldn't believe how lucky he was to have met me, and being with me made him want to be a better man. It was confusing at first when his attention dropped off, but I figured out how to make it work. I figured out how to appear and disappear. Be there when he was ready. I was prepared to wait him out. When Andy sat down next to me on the sand and said hello, I thought this is it. He is the one. Patience. Patience, always.

"Andy!" I call out.

He doesn't hear me.

"Andy!" I call again as I get closer.

He turns, sees me, and his eyes get big. He moves toward me quickly, and I think, he's going to hug me, here, in front of all his friends, but he takes my arm and walks me outside, takes the drink out of my hand and sets it on a table.

"What are you doing here?" he hisses in my ear.

I freeze. Not the reception I was going for. Mouth dry, I try to get it out. "You invited me."

"No, I said I'd call you. I said I'd see you this weekend."

I blink, unable to comprehend what I am hearing. He walks me further until we're outside, coming up again on that group of smokers, hitting the line of cars.

"You said—you called me and said you were coming to Benton for a wedding and you wanted me to come with you," I say, flustered.

"I came up with some friends who don't want me to stay with them at their hotel so they can have some privacy, so I thought I'd crash with you later," he says. "I have to get back, but I'll give you a call. All right? I'll call you in a few hours. I do want to hang out with you, but I gotta do this."

He leans in, gives me a kiss on the cheek. I put my hand where he put his lips, watch him walk away, and feel so gross and pathetic that I want to sink into the ground and never come out. People rush past me, laughing and having fun with each other. Someone bumps my shoulder, and I say excuse me and step out of their way, and they say nothing. Slow and defeated, I walk to my car, get in, and start driving, the road blurry and dark in front of me.

CHAPTER 15

Daniel lives on a dirt road off Lake Mary Road, and the street you have to turn on to get to him is sudden. If you're fiddling with the radio, you might miss it. He was browsing the classified looking for a new house and when he saw where this one was, he said it was perfect. We were at the Hadley's counter, and he got so excited he startled me. This house was quiet, next to the trees, touching nature, perfectly romantic. He wanted to sit on the back patio and drink his spiked coffee and write his lonely sentences. I asked him if he thought the house might be haunted. It's an old house! Old houses are haunted! He was undeterred.

Daniel's front door is unlocked. I open it without knocking. Inside the entryway, The Deer Head wears a green wig. That goddamn creepy deer head. The previous occupant left it on the wall. I wanted him to take it down. Maybe we could bury it. Just think about that poor animal out there enjoying life when some man happens along and shoots it dead. Man v. Nature.

What makes you think it was a man? Daniel asked. Girls hunt too.

So Daniel put the wig on it. For awhile, we called her Josephine but of course it has antlers so it's a buck and then we went back to calling it Dear Head.

He's having a party. I should have driven home. Waited for Andy. Something pulled me here. I wanted to talk. Not to Rebecca. The house is full of people. No Daniel. I see Adrian, Adrienne wearing an unnecessary black lace shirt and jeans so tight I cannot believe she can breathe. A bunch of people outside, smoking. Two girls at the table with markers and sketchbooks. Adrian's marionettes. *Rebecca.* Adrian and I meet eyes first. His eyes are distant and red. His jeans have rust-colored stains on them. Paint, most likely. Blood, wouldn't rule it out. That painting of his own face hangs over the dining room table and people walk past it without paying much mind.

"Hey, Shannon," Adrian says.

"Hello, and hello," I say. "Hello."

Adrienne takes a drink from her glass of water and sort of acknowledges me with a raise of her eyebrows. "Hello Bright Red Lipstick," she says.

The guys then turn to look at me, like really look at me and I freeze.

"Wow," Daniel says, coming out of the kitchen "You look amazing."

He flushes a bright red. Rebecca is still in her hoodie. She's holding a glass of clear liquid. "Hey," she says blearily. She is toasted.

Adrian stands then, walks his marionette over to me. The boy. Corbin. His long fingers work the handle—he calls it German technology—that allows the marionette to lift his arm and tap his black fedora in a greeting.

"Corbin, m'am," the puppet says via Adrian, "pleased to meet you."

Adrian frowns in concentration as he makes him reach out as if to hug someone, then pulls his arms back in like he's decided he's done with the whole business of sincerity. Corbin bobs his head and taps his foot. Besides the gray pinstripe suit and the hat, you can get a pretty good idea of who Corbin is right away; he's the coolest motherfucker in the room. His character is built into his body.

"We're going to make him famous," Daniel says, indicating Corbin.

Flyers cover the table. The puppet show. I take one, put it in my purse.

"You're welcome," Adrienne says.

"Adrienne pulled some strings," Daniel says. "Get it? She has a show at the same time."

A bunch of guys laugh outside, the menacing sound of joy so booming it hurts me for a moment.

Corbin now hangs lifelessly from Adrian's fingers. His head has collapsed against his chest, as though just saying hello to me took the world out from under him. I think I can't stand any more despair tonight. Adrian hangs him where the girl puppet used to be, and now she comes to life. I see she has a new purple streak in her dark hair. She wears a navy-blue dress and red heels.

"Good evening," she says.

I look at Adrian and Daniel. "Say hello to her," Daniel says.

"Seriously?"

She shimmies a little, kind of shakes her hip at me.

"Violet can be feisty," Daniel says.

"She's a bitch," Adrienne says.

She struts to where Corbin hangs. "Baby. Come on. I want to go party."

"I need a drink," I say.

Daniel stands. "Happy to oblige."

I toss my purse on the couch and walk over to the kitchen with him.

"What are you having?" he asks, looking me over again. He opens the fridge.

"A cold beer," I say.

"Make that two," he says and pulls two beers out, opens them with an opener stuck on the fridge.

"Why is Rebecca here? *How* is Rebecca here?

"She had a fight with Gary," he says.

"Obviously. How do you know about that?"

"She told me. She picked up when I called you earlier."

"Right. I was out."

"She told me."

"What did she tell you?"

He nods for me to follow him into the basement. We pass Adrian. Violet dances. Adrienne stretches across the arm of the couch and gives me the eye like she knows something about me I cannot even begin to know about myself. Daniel opens the door to the basement. He pushes the beads aside. I follow him down.

"Jesus, you need a mining hat to get down here," I say at the top of the basement stairs.

A layer of vanilla cupcake scent covers the smell of the old water. They had a flood down here a year ago. Broken pipe. Daniel surges ahead. I stand at the bar. He built it. You can't take this with you when you move so why put out the effort? A pile of clothing is in the corner.

"Those clothes look like a baby elephant," I say.

"A what?"

"A baby elephant. Like a sleeping baby elephant."

"When have you seen a baby elephant?"

"I've seen one," I say and sip the beer. "At a zoo. When I was a kid."

"You're upset," he says.

"An—And aren't I always?" I almost said Andy. Yes, I'm upset about Andy but I stopped myself.

Daniel reaches around me, his weight presses in on me for about a half second, and he turns on a green neon sign that says OPEN. It illuminates a fountain full of ice-water that sits on top of the bar next to a green bottle. I squint.

"What is it?"

As though I've ruined his life by missing the point he says, "Absinthe."

"Absinthe," I repeat. "Where did you get absinthe?"

"You can get absinthe."

Absinthe posters are plastered along the wall behind him. In one, a wild, red-haired woman with a large ass dances inside a green bottle. In another, a green fairy-girl with transparent wings swirls around a table full of people holding glasses and laughing.

"What about the posters?"

"Yard sale."

"The emotional one?"

He pats the bar stools, evades the question but turns on the green emotional lamp. He points to a red velvet couch.

"Did you get that at a brothel?" I sit on one of the stools. It's a swivel stool. I hold onto the bar and move back and forth.

The counter has coasters on it. Cups. And, inexplicably, condiment caddies piled up at the end.

"Stealing from Hadley's?" I ask, pointing.

"He's shuttin' her down. No one will notice."

"You just took them?"

"Yes."

Daniel pats himself down looking for a lighter or matches then he extracts a Bic from his pocket. He slides an ashtray to me. He lights my cigarette. Daniel opens the bottle, pours small shots in the two glasses. He slides the glasses under the fountain, and places two small silver spoons under them. From a white jar with a cork top, he removes two sugar cubes and places them on the spoons, then gently turns two of the spouts. Water slowly drips through the sugar. New shapes form in the green liquid. They're pretty, calming. Daniel makes nice clouds.

"This is called louching," he says.

"Rhymes with douching," I say.

He smiles at me as he comes back around the bar. "You're funny. You know that, right?"

The candle burns. The wax pools toward the wick like worship.

I turn my attention to the bottle and rub the green. "Why the sugar?" I ask.

"The sugar makes it drinkable."

My eyes adjust to the dark. The basement is cold. I cross my arms. Daniel walks around to the other side of the bar and we have music. The Beatles. Sgt. Pepper.

"How's the beer?"

"Delicious," I say.

"You don't like beer," he says.

"I know."

The water. Dripping. Still. Daniel monitors the glasses, which are now half full; he turns off the drip, removes the now empty spoons, and drops a few ice cubes into the glasses. He slides one to me, and then holds his up for a toast. I raise my glass. He raises his glass.

"To new experiences with best friends," he says.

"To good friends who are always there for you no matter what," I say.

He watches me. Eyebrows raised. Body leaned in. Waiting for approval.

"It tastes like medicine," I say. "Is that what it's supposed to taste like?"

He shrugs. "It's supposed to taste like licorice."

It tastes herbal. Not sweet. The sugar, in this case, has taken the edge off but it hasn't wiped away the whole taste. I take a sip and some of it spills on my brand-new wedding shirt. Light green on cotton seems so benign.

"I have a shirt on under this," I say.

"All right."

"I might take it off, throw it on top of the baby elephant."

"You should. You have to let the air out."

"What?"

"You have to let it air out. The stain."

"We should go back up." I sip the drink, try to get acclimated to the taste. "Seriously. Why is Rebecca here?"

"Maybe she's my girlfriend."

"Oh please."

"You don't think Rebecca could be my girlfriend?" He's teasing but he's also not. Daniel taps my glass with his. His body is next to my body. "You're my only girlfriend," he says. "The only one for me."

I move away from him.

132

"Come," he says, and we take our glasses and sit in front of a blank wall. "We have to paint. Find our muse. Open ourselves to our creative space."

He spreads a towel for me on the ground. He sits cross-legged, but I can't because of my skirt. I pull off my nylons, ball them up and throw them on the baby elephant. With a flat head screwdriver, he opens the can of paint to a white glow. Glow in the dark paint.

"You were on a date," he says, not looking at me.

"No," I say and it's the truth.

Daniel waits for me to dip the tip of my brush into the small can. I do so and squint at the wall.

"What am I supposed to draw?"

"Let the muse take you," he says.

He scoots a little closer to me.

"The muse still can't see."

He takes some paint and dots it on the back of my hand and close to me, he says, "Now you're glowing."

I scoot up to the wall, and he mirrors me. I start to draw a monkey. Body, then head, then eyes, then tail.

"You know," he says, sipping his drink with one hand and painting with the other, "absinthe used to have a terrible reputation. Society blamed insanity on it." He writes with his fine-tipped brush *The tiny man sat with his tiny frog on the tiny pier made of black sticks.* "Sometimes that was true. They—the mythical they—made absinthe with crazy things like formaldehyde. People started throwing chemicals together and drinking it and cutting their ears off." He continues writing *the frog talked about how strange the sun looked: unyellow, new orange.* "And a lot of those old absinthe drinkers had syphilis, which, if left untreated, can rot your brain." Daniel pauses and looks over at me. "That's a monkey."

"You sound surprised."

"I didn't know you could draw."

"I can draw."

133

Daniel smiles and goes back to his poem or whatever he's doing. "I think everyone prior to 1950 had syphilis."

He continues writing: *The frogs.*

"A lot of these writers and artists who drank absinthe would hang out together and use the time during which their drinks were festering to talk about high art and society or, you know, hookers they had banged."

"Hence syphilis epidemic," I say.

"Exactly." He glances at my empty glass. "Ready for another?"

"Apparently, you are," I say, indicating his writing. "But yeah, sure."

Frogs, frogs, frogs

"Daniel, what are you writing?"

He leans back and looks at his writing. "Nonsensical bullshit. Life."

He adds a period to the end of the sentence.

"'The first stage of absinthe drinking is like ordinary drinking'," Daniel says, "'the second, you begin to see monstrous and cruel things, but if you can persevere, you will enter upon the third stage where you see things that you want to see, wonderful and curious things.' Oscar Wilde said that."

"And for you, those are tiny men and tiny, worldly frogs."

"One can only hope."

"Stage two sounds awful."

"But you have to get through stage two to see stage three. Mine the dark, scary cave and you might find a diamond."

I stand. "I have to go to the bathroom."

I set my drink on the bar. The bright light in the main part of the house unsettles me, and it seems like people have left. Adrian comes out of his room. He closes the door behind him fast. We have to shuffle around each other so I can get to the bathroom, and he can get to wherever he is going. We're close, Adrian and me. He smells like the outside, like cold and new sweat.

"What are you guys up to now?" I feel much more relaxed than I did an hour ago.

"Adrienne left."

"Oh," I say.

"We had an argument."

"About what?"

He shakes his head.

"Where's Rebecca?"

He nods toward the couch. She's curled up, holding a pillow, mouth open, passed out.

"Daniel is making absinthe."

"I have some reading I want to do," he says.

"Boring."

He scratches his head. "Yeah..."

"Just one," I say.

"Yeah, I'll come down. I'll come."

I'm crampy, like my period is coming, and I almost expect to see it when I pull my underwear down in the bathroom but there's nothing.

Back downstairs, Daniel draws a tree. "It was a queer, sultry summer, the summer they electrocuted the Rosenbergs, and I didn't know what I was doing in New York."

"Oscar Wilde?" I ask.

"Sylvia." He paints another branch. "This is for her."

Adrian walks down the stairs.

"Hey man," Daniel says. "I thought you were otherwise engaged tonight."

"Adrienne left," he says.

"Just hanging out?"

"No, I'll have a drink."

"A drink?"

"Yeah, I'll have one."

Daniel hesitates.

"Just one," Adrian says.

Daniel removes another glass from behind the bar. Three glasses, one under each spigot. Shots. Spoon. Sugar. Dripping. Drip. Rubbing a spot behind his neck, Adrian smiles shyly at me. Drip. My foot is shaking, and I'm swiveling back and forth on the bar stool again so I stop. Drip. I try to be still, stare at the posters, not react.

"My turn to go to the little boys' room," Daniel says and excuses himself.

Adrian sits on the bar stool, straddling it, watching the absinthe.

Drip. Drip. "You know Adrian, I try to be nice to your girlfriend. She's not receptive."

Drip. He watches the dripping.

Drip. "I try to be open to her. Maybe it's not enough."

Drip. He runs his hands through his hair and pushes back from the bar.

Drip. "She's weird to me. I don't know if that's me? Or it's her?"

Drip. He turns completely away from the bar.

Drip. "You shouldn't be with someone you fight with."

Drip. He turns back. Leans in.

Drip.

Drip.

Drip.

Drip. Adrian's hands are on the bar. He has nice hands. Hands that make art. I put my hand over his hand.

Daniel put speakers in last summer. I sat down here with him, and we killed a bottle of some cheap wine that tasted too much like alcohol. That speaker in the left corner, the last one he put in, still looks crooked.

Adrian turns off the drip. He removes the now empty spoons, and drops a few ice cubes into the glasses. He gives one glass to me, and then holds a glass in my direction. "To what's bad for us," he says.

"To what is bad for us," I repeat.

We both drink. We face each other. Adrian has nice eyes. He does. I've said that. Great eyes. I set my drink down.

"You guys had a big fight? Do you want to talk about it?"

"She's just a moody bitch sometimes," he says.

"Humans are fucked up," I say. I don't know why, really, but I put my hands on his thighs and start to kind of rub a little and he lets me, and he is not Andy, and I am not a sad person for chasing Andy, but I am desirable. I pick up my drink again. I am the most desirable.

He gets up and walks to the red velvet cupcake couch. I follow. The space between us is as wide as the gap between the two old seat cushions, worn and threadbare.

"This couch is used," I say, rubbing the cushion.

"It's just a little used," Adrian says.

But I do like the linger, the building-up. The climb where you're going somewhere. Beware vertigo. I put the glass to my mouth. Adrian points to the wall in front of us. More glowing petroglyphs. Frogs with legs coming out of their heads. The frog! Hands like turkeys, like the kind I made in first grade. The turkeys have vaginas for mouths. Their eyes are x's. *Alluring alliteration is an asshole.*

"Daniel is obsessed with frogs," I say. "But look. There. That's an elephant."

His nod is polite and distracted. He finishes his drink in one gulp and I don't think—he sets his glass down.

The absinthe is a new feeling. It's deeper, maybe. Slower. Fuller. It's a mistake coated in candy. Or maybe that's Adrian. Or maybe it's nothing. Maybe it's just alcohol because that's what alcohol does. Takes you away. Gives you permission to be brand new for awhile. I turn to Adrian, take a breath to ask him—but he stands. "I'm getting another round going. But first I'm going to drink Daniel's glass because he's too slow."

My body feels disconnected from my brain. I finish the drink so I can go sit with him. It's so dark down here but that's ok. The dark needs to be a part of this.

I think I feel myself moving up, lifting off the chair, becoming someone interesting. I scoot back and try to put my elbows back on the bar and knock the fountain and that empty glass, Daniel's glass; we're waiting for Daniel.

I take my new drink in both my hands and swallow. I reacquaint myself with my surroundings. Adrian has a loose thread on the bottom of his sweater. I pull it and let it go. We both watch it flutter to the ground and out of sight.

The basement door opens. The beads swing. Daniel says, "Adrian, get your damn hands off my drink."

Daniel swipes the glass from the counter and returns to his spot on the wall. Daniel starts painting again. He draws a lion. I sit near him.

"Do you like that?" Daniel asks and then grins at me.

"Lion slayer!"

Adrian picks up a brush as well. The three of us went to that reading last year. Back when Adrian was healthier. This chick in Raggedy-Ann leggings and a long braid down her back read her revenge poetry and we drank Cokes and ate cookies.

Adrian's paintbrush hovers on the wall, like he just forgot what he was doing. He makes a few marks, then slowly brings the brush down and dips it again in the paint and starts touching up the monkey I made.

"Damn it, that's my monkey."

"Your monkey?" he asks.

"Yes! That's my monkey, and it's a good monkey."

Daniel drops his voice. "Lion slayer, lion slayer, lion slayer!"

We both look at him. That's what the girl in the reading did. She chanted it like that at the end. She chanted for a long time, and no one knew what they were supposed to do with that.

I pick up a paintbrush and try to paint over what Adrian just painted, and he takes my hand and guides it to another spot on the wall. "I'm taking your monkey. It's mine now."

"We've got to get that girl to come read over here," Daniel says, like almost to himself.

Daniel rolls forward so that he's on his hands and knees and touches up the beast he's made. He looks like a little kid. Above what he's drawing, a sentence in Daniel's handwriting. I roll back so I can see it, then read it out loud: *"Wouldn't it be pretty to think so?"*

"Hemingway's zinger," he says.

I point to the next line: *alluring alliteration, an asshole.*

"That's my zinger," Daniel says.

He uses the wall to heft himself up, then reaches out for my hand. I help him up but he stumbles into me.

"Remember those snack cakes? Zingers?" I scoot away from him. "I ate those a lot when I was a kid. That's why I was fat. That's why girls made fun of me. That's why boys didn't like me."

Daniel looks hazily at me, then puffs his cheeks out, then laughs. "I bet you were still cute though."

"My stepdad beat the shit out of me once because I opened a box on a Saturday. I was supposed to wait for Monday. For school. But it wasn't about the snack cakes. It was about following the rules."

Daniel touches my arm, and it startles me so I jerk back and Daniel rather quickly walks back toward the bar like that's what he'd intended to always do. He puts his glass under the drip, flips the fountain on again, then puts the sugar on the spoon under it. Because the water was on first, it redirects off to the side. Daniel doesn't clean it up which is un-Daniel-like. "Don't mind if I do." He pours his little glass full of absinthe, and then just tosses the sugar cube in, and it sinks to the bottom like a lost toy. Adrian is gone then.

"And once again, he drifts into this dark night," Daniel says. "Now I have you all to myself."

Daniel sits on the stool, legs splayed like Adrian was awhile ago, with his hands folded.

"Here is the church," Daniel begins, and he indicates his hands folded over each other. "Here is the steeple." He raises his two pointer fingers. "Open the doors." He pulls his thumbs apart and then twists his hands around, but he's done it wrong. He didn't fold in. He folded out. "And here's all the people."

He's swaying on the chair. Blasted. I haven't seen Daniel this trashed in a long time. He closes his eyes. "They left," he said. "It's empty. See?"

"How much did you drink before I got here?"

We hear Adrian's footsteps above then a door squeaks open and closed.

"Fantastic, he's gone," Daniel says and slides off his stool, stumbles over to the bar and makes himself another drink. "Shit, I can't see shit."

He throws his hand in the air. Behind him. Around him. "We could have all this."

"All what?"

"Happiness?"

"Happiness."

"We could go back to when we first met. Do you remember that?"

"I do. We played pool."

"We did."

He flips the lights on and I blink, hold up my hands in front of my eyes.

He holds his drink up to me then comes back around and puts himself back in his stool then stands, then sits. He puts his elbows on the counter and runs his hands through his hair, over and over. He swivels to me.

"I want to tell you something," he says.

My stomach clenches.

"Daniel," I try to stop him.

"I want to tell you something about yourself," he says, "which is that you are really great. A really great person." He sighs and says in an almost shaky breath. "I like you."

I do not know how to control my breathing. This is what he wants. Is this what I want? Rebecca says to let Daniel in. It's simple. A simple operation. Let Daniel in. Daniel has told me he wants to come in. He told me again before break. He asked me out to dinner. I thought we were going to play pool, but he took me to a fancy Italian restaurant and told me had developed feelings for me, and I screamed in my head. I went to the bathroom and stayed in there for 20 minutes. Then I told him I didn't feel well, and he took me home. Then I left for break and fell back into Andy.

"What do you want?" he asks.

I want to ask him if this absinthe is really absinthe, if what we're doing in the basement is at all original, if my fucked up shit isn't just some version of his fucked up shit and mixing it all together just makes more fucked up shit. But I don't know how to phrase all this without violence.

"I'm a fuckin mess, Daniel. I'm up in Benton, a fucking mess."

He pulls away, and now my instinct is to take him back. The muse says to take him back. Daniel. If I could have chosen my family, I'd have chosen Daniel, and Daniel would save me every day. He'd save me from my stepfather. He'd come into my room and let me cry and distract me with stories, and he'd make me laugh and help me forget the way my stepfather got angry with me for not wiping the counter down the correct way or how he'd pull me out of bed in the middle of the night and make me clean the kitchen, the way he'd make me make fun of my own mother so that he could laugh at her, the way he'd hit and kick our dog in front of us and then not let us console her, and Daniel would tell me he'd protect me, and no one could hurt me because he wouldn't let them, and that's when I'd have to show him my arm, the bruises in the shape of a hand that grabbed me, dragged me into the bathroom to show me the toilet where there was a drop of blood from my period, told me I needed to clean the bathroom because of my disgusting body. I needed to scrub the toilet until all the blood was gone. My mother in the other room with the TV up. The two of us in the same house but different places.

"I'm going to pass out," I say.

Daniel pulls back, too. He picks up our glasses and walks around to the other side of the bar. He turns on the drip again. Another creak from upstairs, and he looks up, and I look up.

"I wonder what he is doing up there," he says.

"What are you going to do?" I ask.

He smiles at me.

"I," he says. "I am going to wait for the curious and monstrous things."

CHAPTER 16

I close the basement door behind me and ball up my fists as though I'm going to hit the wall, but I don't hit the wall. Men hit walls. Adrian comes out of his bedroom, stands in the hall and looks me over.

"I thought you were Daniel," he says.

"I'm not Daniel," I say.

He slips back into his room and leaves the door open.

"Wait," I say. I walk toward him, tap on the door.

The dull light from his lamp casts unrecognizable shadows along his wall. He's hunched over his desk working on rolling a joint. His room is spare and vaguely dirty, not filthy but neglected and wanting. He has another full drink on his desk, nope, half a drink. Nope, he's drank the whole thing. His bed isn't made, and even though it hurts my feelings, I think about Adrienne.

Books are stacked around; clothes are in heaps. Drawers are closed, but not without bits of shirts and shorts and socks and jeans sticking out of them. A guitar case, closed and dusty, sits in the corner.

"Can I talk to you a minute?" I ask.

"Sure," he says.

An empty beer bottle sits on his desk next to the empty glass, next to the magazine. He holds the joint to me. "What do you think?" he asks.

"Nice," I say, turning it around. "Solid workmanship." I hand it back. "You're an artist."

"Nah, the rolling is calming. I don't know. I like it. Something to do with my hands." He opens his desk drawer and in a small black container, he shows me four or five more. I put the one he gave me in my jeans pocket.

"Thanks. I'll save it for a rainy day."

The song changes.

"What's up?" he asks.

143

I lean against his wall. "Everything is fucked up."

"Yeah, it always is."

"Why can't anything be easy?"

"Specifically what should be easy?"

"Guys."

"Oh. Girls aren't all that easy either." He opens his top drawer and pulls out a bottle of whiskey. He opens it and takes a drink then offers me some. "You're having guy issues?"

"Always."

"That guy from Fillies?"

He says it so casually I feel like I have no choice.

"He—well, let me figure out a way to phrase it. He took certain liberties."

Adrian knocks the bottle back. "What do you mean?"

I knock back more. "He just—you know, like forged ahead without checking in first."

He swallows more of the whiskey. Then he seems to get it. "That's really fucked up, Shannon."

I shrug. "Yeah. It is."

Adrian's eyes are red now. He's slurring his words. Adrian puts his head in his hand on his desk. Next to him, the drawer with the joints is still open. He closes it but not before I see a roll of money and bags of pills.

"Does Daniel know you're in here?" he asks.

"Why would that matter?" I answer.

His legs are open, his body is relaxed. I put my arm under his arm thinking I'm going to help him stand up, get him into his own bed where he can sleep it off. His lips are parted just so. When I reach under him to help him up, he stirs, turns to me and lightly presses his lips against mine but pulls back, looks into my eyes and I nod then close my eye, see Andy at that party, the look on his face. When I open them again, it's Adrian. Adrian, who wants me.

He smiles lazily then lifts me slightly, almost pulling me off my feet for a moment. The top of my head reaches his chest. We're swaying a bit, dancing to the music. The feeling of his body is overwhelming. He's rubbing my lower back, then his fingers move up my body.

I kiss him again. He walks me backwards and then we hit the wall, so he has nowhere to put me but up. He lifts me off the ground, and I hook my legs around his waist.

I pause. "You can't hold me like this forever."

"I'm strong," he says. But then releases me and I'm on my feet again.

After a moment, his fingers catch the bottom of my shirt, and he pulls it over my head. He steps back and takes off his own shirt. I click his lamp off. He turns it right back on.

"No," he says. "I want to see you."

"No," I say and again turn off the light.

Sex doesn't matter. It's just the way you feel after, like someone has taken something valuable, and you let them, and in a sick way, you feel good about it because sorrow is what your body craves.

The acoustic music stops, a new song starts. It's a little jazzier. There's bass. But it's similar, I mean, you can tell it's the same group, the same sound, just faster, a little edgier. It will still play for three and a half minutes. Maybe four. Maybe three minutes and fifteen seconds.

His closet door is open. Corbin and Violet hang and wait for Adrian to bring them back to life.

I take his hand and lead him over to the bed, sit him down. I remove my skirt. He looks at my shoulder, the bruise. I redirect. Take his hand and lace my fingers through his, then sit on his lap.

The way he's heating up is not strange. It's the way he keeps looking into me, searching for something, like he's sure whatever he thinks is there is really there even though he can't see it right away.

I stare at a soft space on Adrian's stomach, and I surprise myself by reaching for him, the first place on his hidden self I've touched. He winces, a soft sucking in of wet

air. This animates him. His lips graze my ear. "Tell me what
you want."

It's a question I can't answer because I don't know. I
want him to keep touching me. I want him to know I don't
know how to say that. This is loneliness, I think.

He has a condom. He presses it into my palm. Oh. I do
this. Right. I tear it open, toss the wrapper on the ground. He
unbuckles his belt and slides his pants off and there he is, all of
him, so I slide the condom on him, like, lightly concerned it
might pull or stick on his pubic hair but it doesn't. He guides
me onto him, and I start moving my hips. I'm never on top
with Andy. Never. I close my eyes as Adrian holds my hips
and rocks me. The sensation scares me, being so close and in
control so I move, pull him over and tell him to finish, so he
does. He collapses against me, breathing heavy, and stays this
way so long I start to wiggle away because I can't breathe. He
removes the condom, ties it off and drops it on the floor where
it lands with a soft, wet plop.

Adrian closes his eyes. I stare at him for awhile,
thinking about how he had me against the wall, how I kind of
liked that, how it's over and never coming back. I've always
had a thing for addicts who pay attention to me for five
minutes and then forget I exist. I sit up on my elbows and stare
at him, trace the outline of his body with the glowing paint I
can still see behind my eyes. I slip out from under his arm,
thinking I'll take my things and sleep out on the couch but he
stirs. "No," he says and reaches for me. "Stay."

A sliver of light comes on under the door. Someone is
in the hall. Daniel, most likely. The magnitude of what I've
done settles in and my hands start to shake. But I do as he asks,
I nestle back into him. I wonder if I'll be able to sleep. I can't
sleep when I stay over with Andy. Sometimes he mumbles in
his sleep, and I don't want to miss a moment from his
subconscious. Adrian reaches for me, puts his hands in my
hair, rubs my cheek with his thumb and then stops his hand
heavy on my face. He's passed out. I move his hand back to his

own body. When I close my eyes, I find the spinning chaos, the blackout under the booze that honestly, I don't know why I fight so hard. I curl up inside my head and scream, ball my hands into fists and pound this time, hit the wall, scream *get out get out get out!* Daniel's voice. Get out! Get out! But it *is* Daniel's voice. Daniel's yelling, and I'm conscious enough to pull the covers over me and freeze when he throws the door open, turns on the light and yells louder, "The house is on fire, get out!"

CHAPTER 17

Adrian sits up, confused. Sees me, even more confused. "What's going on?" he says and grabs his shirt and pants, stands up, nearly topples over.

"You go out first," I whisper. "I'll follow."

"What? What?" He stands at his desk, puts his head in his hands. Without looking back, he stumbles to the door and goes into the hall.

"Get out," Daniel says. "Let's go. Where's Shannon?"

He doesn't know I'm here. Oh thank god. Oh thank the good lord. Adrian mumbles something, can't hear him, so I give it a second and rush across the hall into the bathroom and then step out of the bathroom where I run into Daniel, who grabs my arm, shoves my bag and jacket at me, hustles me out into the living room where I stop and see that the back patio is on fire. Adrian registers this at the same time then spins around and rushes back into his room, Daniel after him, me after Daniel because I don't want Daniel to see the condom on the floor, but Daniel is panicked, in go mode, and Adrian wants to save his puppets.

"I called 911," Daniel says. "They're on their way, but we need to get out of the house and get clear of it."

I'm barely alive right now, but I do understand the fire is still outside. The living room is getting smoky, and I can smell the wood burning, the fire trying to spread in every possible direction. Daniel's shoes are in the entryway, so I put those on and rush outside where Rebecca is calling for me from across the street, Daniel and Adrian behind me, Daniel, who has got to still be drunk like all of us, somehow now is a Superman figure, sober and focused, guiding us, telling us to get to the treeline, telling us to go fast.

My entire body begins to shake. It starts from my chest, spreads all the way out. I cross my arms. Sirens in the distance. Oh god it's going to be the hotshot. No, that's only wildfires. This is a domestic fire, *a dom-mes-tic fire,* but does this count as a wildfire because it's going into the trees and the brush and should we—

"Run? Daniel, should we run?" Rebecca asks. She is crying.

The sirens are closer, and over the sirens, from the back of the house, we see the orange glow, the patio destroyed. Rebecca doesn't wait for Daniel to answer, she takes my arm and pulls me back as Adrian sits on the ground saying he's sick, he's fucking getting sick, man, and Daniel is legit concerned about this. He pats his back, tells him sorry, sorry, sorry, sorry, sorry, sorry, so I think this is good, this is fine, he doesn't know, but I am filling up with something new, a mix of deep disgust for myself and my actions and Daniel's soothing voice directed at someone else and not at me. A loud pop, a microburst from the other side, and both of us jump, Rebecca puts her hand over her heart.

The firetruck roars up to the house, and three men jump out, and Rebecca puts her hand on my arm and squeezes, stops crying, intent on them as they pull hoses and put on gear. Daniel rushes toward them, gestures to us, shakes his head yes and shakes his head no, and from some depth of the underworld, offers blankets to Rebecca, to me, and wraps one around Adrian on the ground, who is frozen. I take the blanket. It's itchy and it smells but I am warm again, and the shaking subsides. I walk further away, drop my bag and sit in the dead grass, the silence of the trees behind me ominous and dark, hiding all the things I don't want to see.

Rebecca sits next to me. It is panic or it is drunkenness or it is fear or it is joy but I say to her, "I slept with Adrian."

"Wait, what?"

It is a mistake for her to know this

"You said you slept with Adrian?!"

"No. I said look, Adrian hasn't slept."

Her mouth drops. "That's not what you said."

149

"Fuck," I say and dig in my purse, extract my cigarettes. I find a piece of paper. Daniel's flyer. Adrian's show. I stuff it back in, open my pack of cigarettes and put one between my lips. Rebecca reaches forward, pulls it out of my mouth.

"You can't smoke in a fire!" she almost screams.

The orange glow behind the house gets smaller, then it disappears, and the three men talk to Daniel, their heads bent, nodding, and then a cop car shows up, and the cops get out and also talk to Daniel, and then come over to us but, like, what about the illegal absinthe, and what about whatever illegal drugs Adrian has and do you know Kevin? They want our statements. What happened? I have no idea. I was drunk, and I passed out. With my own full consent, I fucked my best friend's best friend because he's hot, and we've always had a little thing (I thought) and because I thought maybe Adrian would be a safe space, and because, if I am being honest, Adrian seemed into me, but based on his current set of behaviors, I'm not sure he remembers it, and Rebecca goes into the thing with Gary, his cheating, and one of the cops, who somehow is our age, nods enthusiastically and sympathetically and she ends by saying she was just here for some solace with friends, she doesn't know what happened. The cop asks if people were smoking out back. He says there's been some fires from lit cigarettes because of how dry it is, how unusual it is for it to be dry this time of year, how thankful he is that big wildfires aren't the norm, and Rebecca thrusts the cigarette back to me.

"It's hers," she says. "She's the smoker."

"Well, I wasn't smoking on the patio. A bunch of people were smoking on the patio though. There were a bunch of people here," I say.

I'm not the only one making mistakes, is what I mean.

"Do you need a light?" asks one of the cops, and I do. I do need a light. "Just make sure it's out before you walk away."

Yeah, sure. I blow smoke into the air, and Rebecca sighs, swivels between the firefighters and the cops as if she is deciding what to have for dinner, hopefully having forgotten what I told her.

She smiles at me. "I gave that one my number."

"He took our number in the statement."

"Still. I made it clear he was ok to call me."

"You want to date a cop?"

She shrugs. "The Gary thing was a mistake. He made me crazy. Crazy! Though, I started my period this morning. So that explains some of it. Ugh, like I've been feeling insane lately."

The firefighters put the hose back on the truck. Daniel talks to the cops.

"I took some of your tampons" she says, "because I was out."

I inhale the cigarette and let it out. A rustling behind me, so I turn, but it appears it be nothing, or it's nothing I can see.

"You seriously need to clean out under your side of the sink. I sneezed like 80 times."

Another rustling. Maybe an animal? God.

Adrian stands up then, still wrapped in the blanket, ambles toward us, nods to my cigarette, which I offer to him. He says nothing, simply smokes and stares at the house, which, at least from the front, appears intact. Terrified at what's in the back, or what's not in the back.

Somehow I need to tell Adrian the first thing he needs to do when he gets in the house is pick up the condom because maybe I can fix all this. Doubt that Adrian wants Daniel to know, and I certainly don't want Daniel to know. And it's this thought, this image of the full condom tied up on the floor while standing next to Rebecca, who is menstruating, that a pulsing horror begins to take hold, root into my brain where I flash back to walking into my house at the start of winter break, dropping my things in the spare room at my mom's house and going back out to the store to get tampons because I'd started my period, and now, two months later, I realize I have not had a period since then.

The truck's engine revs.

My brain is full of hallucinogenic alcohol, but I attempt the math. So I was home for two weeks, and for sure I had a period. No doubt. Andy and I were together twice. Toward the end of my period when it wasn't totally over but close enough so it wasn't gross. Then again the night before I left. So that's two weeks. I know for sure I started a new pack of pills. I know I took them while I was home because most nights I hung out with my mom while my stepdad was at work, and I wasn't distracted or anything. Then it gets fuzzy. I came back here. All the shit with my car. My birthday. The hotshot happened, what, a week after? Two weeks? And I do hazily recall standing my apartment with Rebecca being like, shit, the pills. Andy. The way he looked at me last night. Or still today? Fuck. I squeeze my eyes tight trying to erase it. He wanted me to leave. He wanted me to be away from him.

The cop rips some paper off a clipboard, and the other cop is back at his car on the radio, and then they're both in their car, also leaving. I put my hand out for Rebecca or for Adrian, but they're not here.

"Shannon?" Daniel calls out for me.

I'm shaking, the blanket gone—Rebecca has both of them.

"We can go back in," he says, standing over me. "Damage to the patio, but not as bad as we thought, and the flames licked the house but didn't get all the way in. Owners have been called, so. I don't know what's going to happen there. You ok?"

"Yes," I say. "I'm fine. But I have to go home."

He offers his hand to me. He face is smudged with ash because the first thing he did when he saw the fire was try to put it out.

"I'm going home," I repeat.

"What? It's the middle of the night."

I walk over to my car and get in, whatever he's saying after me flying off into the night. Daniel in my rearview. He's standing in the road, confused, and I'm sorry for that. I am legitimately so sorry. When I put the car in reverse, I realize I'm still a little drunk, but does that matter anymore? Nothing matters. I get to the end of Daniel's street. The cop car is up ahead, parked off to the side of the road and I can do this, play sober, play normal, play functioning person. I cruise by. They don't do anything. I punch channels on the radio looking for Loveline. Other people's fucked up narratives to get me home, but nothing, just music, because it's Friday. Loveline isn't on Fridays. I dig for my cigarettes then push the car lighter in and wait for it to release.

CHAPTER 18

The Walgreens near my apartment is dark and closed, so I circle the parking lot two times deciding if I want to force this pursuit or give up because it isn't giving me what I want. I pull out. The red of the Safeway sign is a beacon so I go there, park under a streetlamp. I put my keys between my fingers, a weapon if I need it, and leave them out as I walk through the automatic doors.

In my stepfather's house, there's this long, dark hallway, and even though I'm grown up now, it still creeps me out walking down that hall at night. Always feels like something is behind me, coming down on me, and that's the feeling I carry with me all the way to the "family planning" aisle. I glance around to make sure I am alone. No one in this store but me and the cashier, a despondent, middle-aged man with brown hair and a long-sleeved button up blue shirt, wearing a black vest with the Safeway logo on it, reading a People magazine behind his cash register.

What do I know about pregnancy tests? I choose two. The cheapest one, and the second cheapest one. I hold them in my hand, but they don't feel real. Then I put them in my purse, swipe a box of pads off the shelf and tuck them under my arm. I'll make this guy so confused he won't know what to do with himself.

Up front, I stop at the doors, see myself, small and insignificant against the rest of the store in the large mirror. Another glance at the cash register. The man turns a page. Picks up a Golden Delicious. Takes a bite. Chews. I go over to him and put the pads on the belt, then, heart pounding, I reach into my bag and toss the tests on the belt as well. Hilary Clinton and Chelsea Clinton are on the People cover. Only now does he glance at me. He might say hello, but the rush of blood fills my ears, the sound of the ocean canceling out all other noise. I come back into myself long enough to hear the third beep, which means everything has been scanned, and it's over. I ask for a pack of Camel Lights. He has to walk away and go to the lottery counter, unlock the case, then returns with my pack. I ask if he has matches. No, he does not have matches. Gas stations are the places where I'd find free matches.

I write him a check. This whole event took less than five minutes, and relief buzzes through me followed by a light sweat and vague nausea. The hangover setting in while I'm awake.

I open my apartment door but don't turn on the lights and toss the bag on the counter. The red light of the answering machine cuts the darkness in the room. Three messages, I assume, are from Daniel. And I cannot right now with Daniel.

I pour a glass of water in preparation for this test. The nausea gets stronger. I hit the button but it's not Daniel, it's Andy, and I almost spit my water out. Choking, I raise the volume. Andy's voice fills the empty space.

Message 1: *Hey...hey, it's me. Hey...are you there? Can you pick me up?*

Message received, the voice says, at 12:34 a.m.

Message 2: *Hey...it's me. Are you there? I went to my friend's hotel. Can you come get me? They (inaudible). 555-1784.*

Message received, the voice says, at 1:17 a.m.

I am healed. Brought back to peace and light. I dial the number, my heart pounding in my ears. A woman's voice answers. "What?" She sounds exasperated, angry, half-awake.

"I'm looking for Andy?"

Silence.

"He left me messages. Is he there?"

"Who is this?"

"He called and left me a message. I was supposed to meet him tonight. I didn't think—well, he called me earlier, which is how I got this number. Can you get him?" I sound feeble, I know this, and her huff and sigh tells me she's not up for this game. She wants me to stop talking. Or die. I don't know. A loud clunk. The phone gets put down. Her voice in the background. Yelling at Andy. Something-something-crazy-something-obsessive-it's so fucking late and she woke me up (inaudible). Then what sounds like a scuffle.

Andy gets on the phone. "Hey…" he drawls.

His voice collapses me. I sink onto the couch and smile, put my hand over my heart. Thank God. "Hi."

"I can come pick you up," I say.

He reads me the address. I write it down on a piece of newspaper on the coffee table. I know where he is. He's at the Marriott. It's practically down the street. I pick up my keys, my Safeway bag not important right now, and drive to Andy.

I park in the roundabout of the Marriott, then get out and go into the generic lobby. Soft lighting. Everything brown and red. He didn't tell me his room number nor did he say where he'd be if he left said room. I'm prepared to ask the front desk for him. Please call. Tell him I'm here for him because he called for me, but I see him when I walk inside, he's already at the counter, leaning over it, talking to the young woman behind the desk who has her hand on the phone.

"Andy," I say and he turns to me, smiles. "I didn't think I'd see you again tonight."

The young woman assesses me, assesses Andy, but her face is an impasse. I reach my hand to him, but he doesn't take it, instead, puts his arm around my shoulder. His body is warm, musky and overwhelming. He leans into me as we walk outside, where it's cold and silent, the pine trees looming around the hotel. I walk Andy to the passenger side door, but he doesn't get in, just leans against it so I open the door for him and he falls in then turns on his side, toward me. I start the car. Turn on the heat. The seatbelt alarm dings.

"You have to put your belt on," I say to him, but his eyes are closed.

I reach across him, pull the belt down and buckle him in. The alarm stops. Andy reaches forward and turns the heat vents away from himself and onto me. We drive in silence. I don't turn the radio on. Each time we stop, his eyes flutter open and he smiles, then closes his eyes again. I ask him if he had fun at the wedding. I ask him what songs they played. I ask him how long he's known these friends of his.

When we pull up, I tap his arm and he startles, looks at me and smiles, a full and real smile.

"Hi," he says and leans forward, puts his hands on my face, puts his lips on mine, kisses me fully, slips his tongue in. And this is the good stuff. Andy is rarely ever tender. When I'm with him, he's hurried and urgent, which is its own kind of compliment. He pulls away, looks into me, and then tries to crawl across the console but in that process, he leans into the horn with his elbow. The honk seems to shake him out of his trance, and he pulls back, stumbles his way out of the car and slams the door so hard the car shakes. I hurry out and around to him, hooking my arm around his waist. He leans into me, a lovely feeling, until I realize it's because he might fall over, his balance all fucked, and I can't support the weight he is heaving onto me.

"Let's go inside," I say.

He shuffles next to me, laughing, almost tripping walking up the steps until we reach my front door where he leans against the wall, closes his eyes as I unlock it. I take his hand but he stops me.

"God you're hot," he says and puts his hands around me, slides them down my back until he grabs my ass and squeezes.

I push him toward my bedroom where he sits on the bed, and I stand between his legs. Curiously, I'm never forward like this. I wait for Andy to let me know what he wants me to do. Maybe Adrian did something for me. Maybe it was Adrian *wanting* to do something for me. I pull my shirt off and put his hands on my breasts but when I let go, his hands flop down again and he leans back, legs hanging over the side, one arm across his chest, the other splayed out across the bed. He's quiet and unmoving.

"Andy?" I whisper.

I tap his cheek, and his head rolls over.

"Andy," I say in my full voice.

Sighing, I pull his shoes off, line them up next to the door next to mine and play pretend for a full minute what it might look and feel like for Andy and I to live together as a couple. I go into the bathroom, splash water on my face, change into my pajamas and change my underwear. All dried up from Adrian but wet again now.

He's on top of the covers, and when I try to pull them down to slip in next to him, I realize that will disconnect me from his body.

All the times I've spent in this bed alone fantasizing about Andy coming to Benton and now he's here. To my place. To my bed. With my eyes closed, I replay his kiss in the car, how it felt like when we were first together, forever ago. I feel the kiss on my mouth, in my body. I see Andy, then Adrian, then Andy again, then Adrian. Then back to Andy. Then the hotshot, what in the extra fuck, and way back in my throat, I taste the absinthe, sweet now, like Daniel promised. Daniel keeps his promises.

I am pent up, desperate for release, and so I move my hand down my stomach, into my underwear, slip my fingers in and work myself quickly so the release comes fast and quiet. I turn my head into the pillow, panting. I pull my knees into my chest and try to sleep.

CHAPTER 19

Rebecca throws the front door open as I close my bedroom
door behind me, quietly so as not to wake Andy. Her cheeks
are flushed, her hair a mess. She's humming.

"Uh. You're happy," I say.

She smiles and sighs. "I am." She notices my bedroom
door is closed. "Ooh. Who do you have here?"

I pull a mug down from the cupboard. A Hadley's
mug. I turn it around. Did I bring this home and not
remember?

"Andy," I say and then smirk. I can't help it.

She rushes over to my closed bedroom door, and I
walk up behind her. "What are you doing?" I hiss.

"I want to see if he's as hot in person as he is in his
picture," she says and before I can stop her, she cracks the door
and peeks in then closes it. "It's too dark. You sleep in a cave,
it's, like, not good for you. That much darkness."

She flits into the kitchen then and gasps.

"Oh my god, Shannon," she says, eyes wide and holds
up the pregnancy tests.

"I haven't taken them yet," I say and take the tests of
out her hand, toss them back in the bag and shove the bag
under the sink.

"Whose is it?" she squeals but then busies herself with
making coffee.

I shrug.

"Come on, you have to tell me."

Oh, she thinks I'm being coy.

"I don't even know if I'm pregnant," I say but
somehow suddenly with an odd level of self-awareness, I
know that I am, and all at once, I feel all life come out of me,
like some force has used its long fingers to reach in and
squeeze.

"Is it Andy's?" Rebecca asks.

I don't answer. I can't.

I have told myself that Andy wants what I want but he's too afraid to see. He's not ready to embrace our relationship. He needs time to get all his wild out, then he will settle in with me. I have spent the last year and a half readying myself for this.

"I was going to wait for him to leave," I say.

"What? Why? He's here right now."

This could be a push. A little nudge. A little sign. But still. It's not.

"Go take it," she says. She opens the bag and thrusts the boxes at me. "I'm dying."

Fine.

The silence in the bathroom is overwhelming, so I run the water at the sink. I read the first set of directions, then the second. You should take the test with your first urine of the day because of the amount of hormone or whatever. Urine. Jesus. That ship has sailed, so second urine is going to have to be good enough. Great. So I may take these tests and they may be like, we don't know because it's not first urine. First Urine sounds like the name of a nightclub that you can only get into between the hours of 2:30 a.m. and 3.

The instructions seem straightforward. I pee on both of them, though barely and I'm not sure it's enough but I guess we'll find out. I wipe them off with toilet paper and wash my hands, set them on the counter, cross my arms, then chew on my nail. Fuck. My stomach lurches. A monster inside banging on the walls to get out. I check the tests. Nothing yet. I feel insane. Like I could gather all the energy of the earth and scream so loud the mirror breaks. It's only been three minutes. Two lines yes. One line no. Easy. Great. I'll walk away for a second, come back. A watched pregnancy test never ruins your life. I open the door and run right into Andy.

"Holy shit," I say and slam the door in his face.

"Hey, I gotta use the bathroom," he says and knocks.

"Yeah, hold on," I say, frantically gathering the cellophane and packaging.

"Oh hi," a voice says on the other side. "I'm Rebecca, Shannon's roommate. It's nice to meet you. I've heard so much about you."

Oh god.

"Hey," Andy says.

I check the tests again. Nothing. Well. Maybe. I should feel a little more hopeful. Maybe I'm not. But they're not technically done. Am I supposed to move them? Does moving them make them inaccurate? Andy knocks again. No time. I put them under the sink and wipe off the counter one more time, then throw the door open. Rebecca is in flirting position. Hip turned out, pout on.

"Excuse me," Andy says and goes into the bathroom.

Rebecca takes me by the arm and leads me away from the door. "He *is* hotter than the pictures. Omg. You will have beautiful babies!" She realizes what she just said. "Or is that now? I mean. If, you know. You know what I mean."

From the bathroom, Andy calls out, "You're out of toilet paper."

"Oh ew," Rebecca says and puts her hands out in a stop motion. "He just gets up and takes a shit in our bathroom? Minus five on the hot scale."

"Yeah, it's under the sink," I yell to him.

"What happened on the test?"

"I don't know yet. It was still going."

"Did you leave them out?"

"No, they're under the sink." I freeze. Oh shit. What is wrong with me? "No, actually, I can get you some. It's not under the sink."

Andy is quiet.

"Andy?"

The toilet flushes. The water runs. But he doesn't come out.

Rebecca hovers. Both of us, waiting.

"What's he doing?"

I don't know, but my heart has stopped beating. The door handle turns, and I shove her away. "Go. I have to talk to him. Go, go."

Andy walks out. He blows past me, picks up his shoes that were so lovely sitting next to my shoes and sits on the edge of the bed to put them on. I sit next to him, trying to take up the least amount of space. My mouth is dry, and I can't make words.

He stands. "Can I use your phone?"

Finally, my voice returns. "Do you need to go somewhere? I can take you."

"Nah, I'll call my friend." He picks up the phone, dials a number from a piece of paper from his pocket and turns away from me.

I go back into the bathroom. Everything appears in place? The toilet paper is on the counter, a piece of it fluttering down. Old roll left behind.

From the other room, I hear Andy's voice. "I don't know man. I was out of it. I have no idea where I am. Hold on."

I squat down, open the cupboard. The tests are where I left them. The tests are done.

Andy pops his head in, registers me holding the tests, and some insane, brief flicker of light flashes across his face.

"Andy, wait," I say, but he's in the living room, asking Rebecca for the address, which she gives him and is clearly confused as to why he's asking her.

"Thanks," he says and almost gives me a small hug but stops, pulls back and tries to get out the door but it's dead bolted. Rebecca steps forward and helps him open the door. I give her a dirty look.

"Wait," I say and follow him still clutching the tests. I'm only wearing socks, and the ground is ice. I don't put on a coat.

He walks far away from me, stands in the parking lot looking around for, I assume, his friend he called to get him.

"I thought maybe—

But he cuts me off. "You are not my problem," he says.

A car pulls in through the broken gate. Andy begins waving at it.

"Can we talk about this? Can we just talk about it?"

A woman is driving. She looks out at me in sunglasses. Maybe she's the woman from yesterday. His friend's girlfriend? He gets in the door and indicates this woman should drive away, which she does. He does not wave. I stand behind the car and watch him go.

Numb, I go back inside. Rebecca is standing at the door. She glances at my hand, and I hold the tests up to her.

Two lines. Pregnant.

"What are you going to do?" she asks.

My purse is on the floor, and I rip through it, open my wallet and call the number on the back of my credit card, the new one, to check the balance. $89 available until I reach my credit limit. $10 minimum payment due next week.

"Shannon?" Rebecca repeats.

I stare at the wall in front of me. There's a poster up of a desert scene. My mom gave it to me before I left for college to remind me of home. Home = cactus, a sunset, flowers.

Rebecca puts her arm around me. "I need you to know something."

Rebecca has her issues. She's entitled and spoiled. A great singer! Often emotionally tone deaf. But she's been a good friend. She lets me live here for a quarter of the rent. I'm grateful right now for her.

"I slept with Daniel last night," she whispers. "Or. I guess. Technically this morning. After you left."

I shake my head.

She bites her lip and nods. "And, yes, it was amazing. You seriously missed out."

The phone rings then. It's my mother. Leaving Rebecca on the couch, I take the phone into my room and close the door.

I stare at the outline of Andy's body in my bed as my mother says hello, my stepfather has run out to the store, and she has a few minutes.

"I'm so sorry," she says, her voice almost breaking. "I haven't had a chance to talk since we were up there."

I sit on the opposite side of where Andy had been.

"I know," I say. "It's ok."

"He's a lot," she says. "I know that."

I lean forward and smell the pillow. Smells like his shampoo.

"But he's good to me," she says. "And your father." She sighs. "He was awful. Just awful."

"I know," I say. "Really, Mom, you don't have to explain."

"I do though. Honey. I'm sorry. I know what we talked about, and I'm sorry. I am."

Andy and this outline. His shampoo. His smell. I strip off the pillowcase. Cover the naked pillow with the blanket. The action of this feels final. In a real way. I've quit Andy before. But he kept coming back. Calling me. I once told him I was in love with him. He kissed me after I said it, but he didn't say it back. I thought it meant he loved me too.

Rebecca is in the other room singing so loudly I can hear her all the way in here with the door closed.

"Mom, I have to tell you something," I say.

"Honey, one second," she says and the line is muffled. "The garage door is coming up. I need to go."

"Wait," I say and feel panicked. "Wait, don't hang up. Listen. I'm…I'm…"

"Honey, can you call me back in a few hours when he goes to work?"

"Mom, no. Hold on. I'm pregnant."

On the other end of the phone, I can hear my stepfather's voice asking who she's talking to, and she says me, and he asks her to go out and get the bags from the car.

"What?" she whispers.

"I'm pregnant," I say quickly.

"Shannon," she says, and I can hear she's almost in tears.

"Can you come here?" I ask, now my voice breaking. The sorrow overwhelms me, and I sit on the floor and lay down, lay my head on the receiver, hearing my mother's breathy voice, hurriedly trying to soothe me before my stepfather makes her get off the phone.

"I'll give you a call later on, all right?" she says, her voice full now so I know he's there.

"Mom, don't tell him. Promise me. You can't tell anyone."

I sit with the phone in my hand for at least a minute and then it rings again. Daniel, caller ID says. I'm about to answer but it stops. I pick up the line anyway and hear Rebecca chattering to Daniel and then she's quiet.

"I got it," Rebecca says.

Daniel doesn't speak.

"You can hang up, Shannon, I got it."

The floor feels safer. Within moments I'm sobbing, heaving so hard I feel as though I'm going to throw up and then I am, I am throwing up, head over the toilet bowl, the lingering stench of Andy making me vomit even harder.

When I'm finished, I wash my face and brush my teeth then drag myself into the living room and paw through my bag for my cigarettes. Rebecca is giggling into the phone. She eyes me and puts the phone against her shoulder.

"Should you be?" she nods toward my cigarettes.

"Oh god," I say and go outside and light up with a shaky hand, inhaling as deep as possible, wanting all of it inside me then I exhale with a shuddering breath. I ash on the ground, note, continuously, the ashtray is overflowing.

A headache rumbles behind my eyes, clouds gathering, but maybe all it is, is the lack of caffeine. Maybe sometimes all you need to fix yourself is coffee. Rebecca is off the phone. She watches me pour coffee and then rummage in the fridge for creamer, which we again don't have, and so I use the Bailey's.

"I—Shannon. Listen. If you need something, let me know, ok?" she says. She lingers for a second, but I notice now she's dressed to go out. This paralyzes me. I sip my coffee in hopes the liquid will ignite. I haven't warmed up from being outside earlier.

"You can't tell anyone," I say. I catch myself. A lump in my throat. I feel confused and uncertain and disoriented. Because then I have to add, "Not Daniel."

"Oh god. I wouldn't tell Daniel."

"Where are you going?"

"I have a test this week. I was going to the library."

I shouldn't care if she fucked Daniel last night. This morning. Hours ago. I walk to the couch and sit. Sore, a little, from Adrian.

She sits next to me. "You ok?"

"I don't know."

"What are you doing to do?"

It is so quiet in the apartment I can hear her watch ticking.

"My cousin had an abortion," she says, whispering even though we're alone. "It was like $400."

Coffee. Coffee. Sip, Sip. The caffeine and the little bit of alcohol clash. The fight feels good.

"Well, then she also had a baby the next year. Different guy though."

"Not helping," I say.

She picks at a thread on her flannel. "All right, well, let's not talk about that right now. I seriously need you to know how amazing Daniel is at sex."

And then she proceeds to tell me how it all went down. After the firefighters left—she wonders if one of them will call because she gave him her number—they went back inside and Daniel was distraught. Like, insanely distraught. Raw and open.

"I guess your house burning down will do that to a person," she says. "By the way, the whole house stinks. We were like, should we leave? Should we go somewhere? But, like, no one wanted to drive so I guess we just hung out in the lingering smoke."

Adrian went back into his room, closed the door. Daniel sat on the couch and put his head in his hands, and Rebecca sat next to him, patted his shoulder, and then she hugged him, and then—Rebecca smiles mysteriously, like she's unlocked the secret to the universe—they were kissing.

"He was insistent. Like, hungry. You know, Gary. Jackhammer. Get in, get out. Daniel though. Wow. Like, he had fire in him. Excuse the term, you know. He literally swept me off my feet. Just had to have me right there. It was wild. We were on the couch." She lowers her voice. "Adrian could have come out at any second."

She says he went down on her right there, and she had an orgasm almost immediately. She's never experienced anything like Daniel. Who would think? She laughs. Daniel. I mean, Daniel? Oh my god. But really, he is secretly kind of hot? Again, haircut, take a little better care of himself. Dress in clothes that flatter him. Etc., etc. The sex though? Not sex. The fucking. The animalistic fucking.

"Like, he was literally taking it out on me, and he was welcome to do so," she says and leans back, closes her eyes as if she's reliving it all and I finally stand up, go into the kitchen and pour half my cup with Bailey's and the other half with coffee.

She cranes her neck on the couch, "Do you want to have dinner tonight? I have a Quizno's coupon."

"Yeah, sure," I say. The bread sounds appealing, but the meat inside does not and another wave of nausea hits but I swallow it back, trying to command my body for a change.

She grabs her backpack. Surprises us both by giving me a hug. Then walks out the door.

I go pick up the mail. Two bills. Two credit cards now. One past due. I turn on the TV and sit on the couch, thinking the coffee and cigarettes will keep me up for hours but, then, of course, I only slept three hours last night and soon I'm out and then waking to the sound of the phone ringing. The light outside is gray now. Day gone.

"Hello," I say.

"Honey, did I wake you?" My mom.

I sit up. "No. I mean, yes, but it's all right. It's all right." I look at the clock. Past 5. Jesus Christ. Disoriented and groggy, I try to stand up but feel dizzy, so I sit again.

"How are you?"

"Fine. I mean. Not really fine, but you know."

I rub my eyes and try to get my bearings. I'm thirsty, so I stand again, slowly and take the phone into the kitchen where I pour myself a glass of water and drink it.

"All right, so, I have a plan. There's a plan for you," she says.

This brings me fully awake. I am saved. She's going to come up here with the money, and we'll do this together.

"Mom," I say. "Thank you. I cannot even express how thankful I am."

"So," she cuts me off. And it's then I can hear her smiling in the phone. The Bill smile. Again, I look at the time. He should absolutely be at work. "What if, now, hear me out, but what if you come here?"

"What?" I whisper.

She repeats herself. "What if you come here?"

"I mean, I heard you, but," I say. "Do you mean come to Phoenix to get the abortion?"

"Oh no, no, I mean, no. No, no. I mean, come here. Come home. You can have the baby here."

My cigarettes in hand, I step out and light one, blow the smoke away from me toward a man walking, who dramatically waves his hand in front his face. I feel her hesitation on the phone, and I'm nervous now.

"Wait. Is Bill there?"

In a rush, she says, "Bill and I think it would be lovely for you to come here and have the baby."

"The *baby*?" I suck in half the cigarette and cough.

"Calm down. Honey, calm down. Bill says it would be fine, and we'd love to help you," she says. "Really, it's a little exciting. Not the way I imagined it for you, but I think—"

"You told Bill?" I shriek again.

And it's then I hear a little noise on the phone. A little breathing or I don't know what he's doing.

"Bill?"

"This will all be ok honey. I promise," she says.

"Bill," I say again. "You told Bill."

"Honey, I had no—yes, because he's—he's here and ready to help."

"I told your mother to expect this kind of thing," he says. "I knew it was coming. That girl's gonna get knocked up and she's going to end up right back here."

The cigarette burns between my fingers. I feel frozen. Paralyzed. Listening to his judgment, like I'm 12 again sitting at the dining room table. Bill saying he's going to make me sleep outside to learn to appreciate how good I actually have it at home. Me awake in the middle of the night, panicked that the couch cushions weren't straight. Bill making me change my clothes before school because I looked like a slut. Bill making me sit down and detail every second of every minute I was out of the house. Me sitting down at the kitchen table with a detailed plan for a movie night with my one friend and then Bill telling me I can't go anyway. Bill walking up behind me, yelling in my face, spitting all over me, that the rocks I was supposed to clean off in the driveway are still there. Bill hitting the dog. Bill hitting me. Bill making us wait on him. Can I get you another soda? Can I get you a snack? Can I get you your cigarettes? Do you need a lighter? My mother, sitting there through all of it, grabbing me as I came home from school to give me a Bill Mood Report. If he was in a bad mood, if he was already boiling about something, the best course of action, my mother taught me, was to give him a hug, ask him how he was feeling, offer him help in some way. Keep him happy, my mother always told me, and then we get to be happy. The cigarette has burned all the way down, and the heat is too close to me now. I snap.

"Get off the phone, Bill," I say.

My mother nearly gasps.

"Hang up, Bill," I say. "I want to talk to my mother."

"Now—

"Hang. Up. The. Fucking. Phone. Bill!" I scream and another person walking by stares at me. "Hang up the fucking phone! Hang up the fucking phone!"

"Shannon," my mother says but there's a click and I know he's off.

I have exactly 13 seconds before he's up in the living room yelling at her.

"Listen, Mom. Listen to me. I'm not coming home. I'm not. I'll get the money some other way. But I can't believe you told him. I can't believe it."

"Shannon," she says, defeated. "I can't believe *you* right now."

All I hear now is the dial tone.

CHAPTER 20

This guy named Tuck taps my arm, and I wake up, realize I've dozed off behind a computer in class. The prof is roaming around, stopping occasionally to look at people's screens, oohing and aahing or making comments. We're supposed to be making a mock ad for Jif peanut butter. I have a blank screen. Tuck's skateboard is under the desk. He has long hair in a ponytail and wears big t-shirts. His backpack is in tatters, held together with pins. I think Tuck is his last name. Tucker. Or maybe Tuck is his first name. Tuck nods over to the professor. Who, yes, told us all to call him Gus, everyone calls him Gus, but I have not called him that nor do I plan to call him that. I peek at Tuck's screen where he has, surprisingly, designed a beautiful ad for Jif. A family sitting around a table eating peanut butter and jelly sandwiches. A mom and two kids. No Dad. Where is the dad? No one ever knows where the dad is in the Jif commercials.

Class is over. Everyone starts turning off their computers, and I do the same but Gus calls my name, asks me to stay after.

Gus is a tall man, lightly imposing. Bald, wearing a blazer with patches on the sleeve. I brace myself for a pep talk. A lecture. And my response is going to be an assurance I will try. I will tell him this isn't who I am. I get good grades. I follow the plan. I will tell him I don't totally know what's happened to me, or why I'm doing all of this to myself other than the real hard truth is that I need it because that's what I was taught.

But all Gus says is this: "Stop sleeping in my class."

It's a slap.

Then he turns to the front of the room to gather his things.

I walk outside toward my car to go to work where I plan to, once again, ask for more hours or a raise. This morning when I put on my pants, they felt tight, and I looked at myself in the mirror, at my puffy face, and realized I am out of time.

When I walk into Neighborhood Insurance, Carmen is clicking something on her mouse and glances at me. I'm barely at my desk—my bag is still around my shoulder—and Marie pops her head out of her office.

"Shannon?" she says and nods for me to come in.

She's at her desk next to the window. Beyond her, I see people walking two by two or in groups of three. People happy with their lives. Enjoying each other. No bullshit. No drama.

I sit in the leather chair.

"Can you please close the door?"

I stand again, close the door.

She leans forward, her hands clasped in front of her.

I wonder if someone has died. If someone has quit. For three seconds, until I finally register the sad smile she gives me is not because she has some earth-shattering good news about a promotion or more money but because she feels sorry for me.

"Shannon, I've noticed you've been checked out here for awhile. You called out twice last week. I'm honestly surprised you're here today. I see you on your computer checking your personal email."

God, I knew she was spying. I knew all those times she cruised my desk she wasn't going to get water. Sometimes Daniel forwards me funny things. Or sends me little stories about a guy named Darren who works nights at a place called Jack's Diner and all the customers he meets and interacts with.

My face is red. I can feel it. I'm burning up. I open my mouth to defend myself, but nothing comes. I'm so taken off guard that I can't form words.

I'm not supposed to be a person who gets fired.

I'm not supposed to get called out for sleeping in class.

Marie picks up an envelope and taps it on the desk. She has a stack of Popular Mechanics on her desk.

She slides the check to me. "This will be your last check. We wish you the best."

She stands then, folds her hands in front of her. Slowly, I rise and open the door. I stop.

"Do you want me to close it again or leave it open?"

Marie has taken a seat again. She's writing something on a piece of paper and doesn't look up. "Leave it open, thank you."

I slowly walk to my desk. I don't have anything personal over here, but I take a pen. It's my favorite pen. Blue ink. I use it all the time. I walk through the lobby, and another young woman is standing there engaging with Carmen. Marie walks out then too, glances at me, calls the young woman back.

Outside, I open my last check. $56.

I drive to the bank and deposit it and pull out $10 to fill up my car.

With nowhere else to go, I drive to Hadley's. The parking lot is empty. The big sign says: THANK YOU BENTON! But the N is gone.

The doors are locked. Maybe he's in the back, but I can't see him. I peer in. It's a mess. Boxes out. The counters full of plates and silverware. Garbage bags everywhere.

I open my purse for my cigarettes and as I'm shoving everything around to look for them, I find a wadded up Hadley's napkin with a number on it. Adrian. I go over to the payphone and page him. That wad of cash in his drawer. I mean, it's from drugs but—

The payphone rings.

"Adrian," I say as I grab the phone back up.

"Who is this?"

"It's Shannon," I say. "I need some help. Where are you?"

"I'm at the house," he says.

"I'll be there in 15 minutes," I say and hang up.

At Daniel's house, I park on the street, not in the driveway. The garage door jerks up, catches, reveals half a body, jerks up again and then Adrian is fully realized. He holds the door up with both hands to make sure it doesn't come down again—their garage door is a mess. It never stays where it's supposed to stay. He wears jeans and a long-sleeve flannel and fingerless leather gloves. He sees me and stops, arms still up in the air, palms open ready to catch the door in case it falls but it doesn't. I hold up a hand and wave. He waits a beat before he waves back.

"Hello," I say.

"Hello," he says.

Behind him, Daniel's car.

"Is Daniel here?" I ask.

"No," he says. "He let me use his car but he's out—he's at practice."

"Practice?"

"The show."

"Right."

He walks out, away from the garage door. We have two bodies of space between us, then just one. I take a settling breath but it does not settle me, and I understand, more and more, how impossible a task it is to feel settled. He brushes past me and disappears around the side of the house. I smell the patio before I see it. They've torn it down. A pile of blackened wood in the grass away from the house. Black streaks spread out on the house. It is still unclear what damage was done to the inside. Adrian grabs a piece of wood from the damaged pile and walks toward the garage. He situates the board across two wood horses and opens a can of red stain.

"What are you doing?" I ask.

"Building the stage."

"For the marionettes?"

He nods but doesn't look at me. The chemical smell replaces the burn. Behind him, a radio is on. Stone Temple Pilots.

"Do you have any cigarettes?" I ask.

"I do," he says and turns back into the garage.

I walk under the garage door and hold up my hand in case the stupid thing crashes on me. Daniel makes fun of me when I do that. He'd turn and grin at me and say I was too easy to scare. I'd tell him I was protecting myself. The garage door is not the real problem.

Adrian has a corner in the back where he stores his old oversized, unused canvases. Looks like maybe it's a functioning space now with half a storyboard taped up on the wall—the puppets drawn in pencil in different positions, some touching each other, some of them alone. Cigarette butts litter the floor. Next to the butts, a dustpan holds more butts and a broom rests nearby. Old towels, stiff and crusted from dried paint, sit resigned on the bottom shelf of the workbench. Daniel made the work bench a few months ago from scrap someone dumped in the woods behind his house.

Adrian tosses me a soft pack of Camel Lights that only has three cigarettes left. I pat my pockets. Adrian offers a light. A Zippo. An old one. Like the hotshot's Zippo. He pops the lighter open with his thumb, the metal scrapes against metal, and strikes the flint wheel but it doesn't catch.

"Wait," I say. "Is it going to ignite the vapors in the air?"

He laughs a little then tries a second time. The flame jumps. I lean in for it. After lighting his own, he snaps the lighter shut with a click. Because of where we stand in the garage, the cigarette smoke doesn't have much choice and collects in the air around us forming a haze.

He turns the Zippo around in his hand then stuffs it in the front pocket of his flannel, the weight of it causing unbalance in his shirt. Adrian leans against the workbench, and his weight makes the wood creak and shift. The cigarette hangs between his fingers like it gives no fucks. A rusted rake hangs off the wall.

"So," I say. "Anyway."

He brings the cigarette to his lips and takes a drag and exhales.

175

"How's Adrienne?"

He shrugs his shoulders then checks his watch. "Adrienne is on her way," he says.

"That's awesome," I say. My voice is two octaves higher but I can't help it. "Awesome. So you guys are good."

"Why wouldn't we be?" He puts the cigarette between his lips and goes back to work, dumps some stain on a rag and begins staining the board.

I smoke fast, like take three drags in a row. "I don't know. There's no reason. Of course you're good."

"You said you needed help?" he asks without looking up.

"Yes! Yes. I need some help."

He pauses now.

"I need help," I say again. I rub my eyebrow and stare down at the floor, dotted with red from the stain. "I need to get something. That costs money I don't have. And I don't know how to get that money."

He goes back to staining. "What do you need to get?"

"Uh—I need to." I gesture down at my stomach. "Uh, have something removed."

"What?"

"A, um. Something that—you know that old joke about a wire coat hanger?"

He shakes his head, thoroughly confused.

I sigh. Lean closer and whisper. "I need to have an — an." I stop. "I need to have a procedure. A medical procedure."

He stares at me, still not getting it.

"Jesus, Adrian. I need to have an abortion." I watch his eyes get wide and I reach out with my hands like, no wait, don't freak out. I turn behind me, but we're still alone. "You can't tell anyone. You can't tell Daniel."

I can see Adrian's face, in his brain, he's doing the math, trying to figure out when we were together, just a few days ago, and I can tell from the way he frowns and starts to sweat what he's thinking, no, statistically impossible based on

176

a hundred different reasons not to mention he used a condom, but I do not correct him or reassure him.

"How much do you need?" he asks.

"Um. It's, like, um, $500."

"Holy shit."

A car pulls up in the drive. Adrian turns away from me. A door slams. Adrienne's voice. "Babe?"

"Shit," he says.

"I got my pictures in the back of my car—oh," she says when she sees me.

Oh could mean anything. She knows. She doesn't know. She hates me. She's indifferent to me. She's surprised to see me in the garage without Daniel home, talking to her boyfriend.

"Hey, Adrienne," I say, way too enthusiastic. Keep it down.

"Hey," she says, like she's acknowledging a nuisance.

Adrian puts his arm around her and hugs her in greeting. She hugs him back, and he kisses her on her mouth. She reaches up to his mouth and wipes off her lipstick. "You know, red is kind of your color," she says.

Her black, lace-up boots go to the middle of her thigh.

"I love your boots," I say, "those are cool."

She glances down at herself.

"Where'd you get them?" I ask.

She turns to me like a fly has been buzzing around her and she just can't stand it anymore. "Why? Are you going to go out and buy them?"

I keep my enthusiasm at a level 10. "I just like them a lot. I think they're really great."

"Can you help with my pictures in my car?" she asks Adrian.

His fingertips are stained red. She picks up his hand and holds it up to him. He takes his hand back, she gives a disapproving snort and goes back to her car. I take his arm and he turns to me. I open my eyes wide. I'm begging. Adrienne yells his name again and he follows.

She piles poster boards into Adrian's outstretched arms. He must be holding eight. Nine. Ten. Eleven. Twelve. I stand there like an idiot try to look what's on them and she notices this, steps between us.

Adrienne removes the final five. She kicks the car shut with her foot. "Shannon, can you grab the door?"

"Yes, yes, happy to, sorry," I say.

Adrienne goes in first and Adrian after, and I have to shift around to allow him space to get in, and we brush against each other. He's sweaty, damp. Warm. He moves then and an edge of the poster board pokes me in the arm, leaves a mark.

I'm inside the house now in the daylight, which always feel strange. Deer Head wears a Benton State hat.

Adrienne and Adrian are talking, heads together, low so I can't hear and then Adrian glances at me, almost apologetically.

"Shannon, you said you wanted a drink?" Adrian calls out to me.

I go to him in the kitchen. He opens the freezer door and removes a coffee can, pulls out a bag of marijuana and a wad of money.

"This is my cold cash," he says.

The money smells like pot. I stuff it in my pocket. He seals up the can, shoves it back in the freezer. Goes into the living room and leaves me alone in this kitchen I've spent so much time in with Daniel. Laughing. Making drinks. Eating pizza in the middle of the night. Telling each other stories.

I walk toward the door. Adrienne glances over her shoulder. She lifts her hand and waves me off. Shoo, she says. Shoo, shoo.

CHAPTER 21

We're in the dark, sitting in the car. Hot coffee steams next to me. It's not mine. I'm not supposed to eat this morning. Another car pulls up near us, and an older man gets out, walks around to the back of his car, opens his trunk, and removes a large posterboard. He slams the trunk. Picks up his board. Walks toward another man and woman who are standing by the side of the building. This isn't as terrifying or awful as they made it out to be at the first appointment, but still I feel panic, and more than anything, I want it over.

"You can't tell anyone," I say.

"I know. You already made me promise."

"I mean it. Not your mom. Not your best friend from first grade. No one. Promise."

"I already promised you! I'd never tell anyone about this."

"Please! Promise me again! You can't tell anyone!" I am near tears now and Rebecca puts up her hands.

"I'll take this to my grave."

"I'm scared," I say.

"They do this all the time."

The door opens. A woman emerges. The people hovering animate like zombies and surround her. She rushes up to the car, opens my door. Rebecca sticks a jacket in my face, which I put over my head. Rebecca on one side, and the woman from Planned Parenthood on the other, hustle me in the door as the three protestors screech at me that I am a murderer, and God will punish me.

The woman locks the door, sighs, and as I take the jacket off my face, asks if I'm okay. She motions for us to follow her. We're led into a waiting room. Another girl sits against the wall. She is alone, barely awake, and is very young, like for sure she needs an adult consent here but then an older woman comes back, holding a Styrofoam cup of coffee that she blows on. She sits next to the girl but does not say anything to her, or hold her hand or offer any sort of comfort, and the girl must sense me looking at her and we make eye contact, I smile, and she goes back to staring at her lap.

I go up to the front desk, which is behind a plastic shield, and the woman gives me some paperwork through an opening along the bottom of the shield. There is a questionnaire about my life habits that I don't want to answer, but I answer questions about my medical history, family history. I sit in one of the black plastic chairs that line the wall. Instead of magazines on the tables, brochures are stacked on top of each other. Rows and rows of Facts and How to Get Help and What You Need To Know and cards for websites — lots of cards for websites and hotlines. HPV: Facts. The Pill: Facts. A book on the side table called *I Never Called It Rape*.

A domestic violence brochure. I pick it up. A child — a girl, it's *always* a girl — is on the cover. Her head is in her hands and she's looking sullen. sitting at a desk or something. I open it. Inside it says: I'm afraid.

I close it. Put it back. Stare at the wall in front of me with posters about STDs.

I bring her the paperwork. She asks me for the money. I give her the cash that smells of marijuana, but we both pretend like it doesn't. She smiles, like she's grown weary of the bullshit. I stare at her wedding ring finger with what looks like an engagement ring on it, a big diamond surrounded by two smaller diamonds on each side. Someone loves her. Wants to be with her forever.

"I like your ring," I say.

She uses her thumb to turn it slightly, like she had forgotten what it felt like. "Thank you. They'll come get you in a few minutes."

The young girl is gone, but the woman remains, and Rebecca pats the seat next to her, so I sit and try to calm down with deep breaths. I'm not hungry, in fact, I feel sick. I have smoked no less than 1000 cigarettes since last night.

The same woman who led me through the protestors calls me back. I follow the woman and try to pay attention to what she's saying. She tells me her name is Jane. She hands me a pink gown, explains, again, about the procedure, the suction, the cramping and bleeding that will follow, like a heavy period, the risks of infection, the need for birth control.

"Any questions?" she asks.

"No, I just want this to be over," I say.

"It will be," she says, soothingly.

I strip down. My sweatshirt. My bra. My sweatpants. Last, my underwear. A doctor, a woman, and another staff person, another woman, gather round me. They are in scrubs. I lie back on the bed. My feet go up into stirrups that have yellow oven mitts over them. One, then the other. This room, it's all white. All quiet now. Kind voices. Reassuring.

In my mind or in real life, the word father is mentioned, and I hear a woman say, "No, he is not important."

And the doctor says, I'll tell you what I'm doing before I do it, ok? You're going to have sensations, and you're going to feel some things, ok? You'll feel tugging. You'll hear noise. The noise may be loud.

No. I want to drift. I want to sit in my mother's garden, the one she had before we moved out here. I close my eyes. Try to take myself away.

The neighbor boy I had a crush on plucked a strawberry off the vine. His kid fingers were mushy. He blew on the berry for me. The sky was sepia toned. Tornado season. We had a basement. Sometimes the basement flooded. My mom kept a large bag of potatoes on the stairs.

Cold air pulls me back. Exposure. I tense up. Relax, it's ok, relax, they all say to me.

I ate the strawberry because he wanted me to. When we were finished, he plucked another one off the vine and gave it to me. I ate that one, too. He laughed. He pulled another and another. He said to put them all in my mouth—it was funny. I puffed up my cheeks. Tried to swallow. So thick. But I did it.

We heard our mothers calling. I was sticky. My fingers were red. My mouth was red. Bits of seed and dirt smeared my cheeks. My mother brought me inside to clean me up. My stomach hurt. Too many strawberries.

The tugging. A lot of tugging. Noise. My eyes are still closed, squeezed shut now, like I'm about to go down a roller coaster. The tugging makes a sharp turn to a pinch and then pain; a deep, incredible pain that takes root in my nerves, travels down to my knees, into my back, up through my shoulders, and I want to squirm back, pull away, but I am forced to stay and witness this event with my body. I open my eyes, and my mother and I are at the sink together. She wet a paper towel and cleaned my face, told me she liked the neighbor boy, wanted to know if I liked the neighbor boy, did I think he was cute, how exciting, my first crush, though it didn't matter because we were leaving our home, going on a big adventure—what did I think of that, she wanted to know. You and me, she said. Just us. Just us, she said, and the noise gets louder, as loud as anyone can imagine, and the doctor is talking, but I don't know what she's saying anymore because I'm trying to find Daniel's voice. The two of us before winter break. The two of us before he ruined everything.

You're breaking the rules, Daniel! You are hurting me by breaking the rules of this friendship, and it's not my fault. Your feelings for me are a betrayal. Daniel's face blurs away and that will haunt me forever as the doctor tells me it is over. But it doesn't feel over.

I'm panting. Emptied. Tears are running down my cheeks, but it's relief.

Jane hands me off to Rebecca with my bag of clothes. I'm wearing a big pad. Watch for infection. Take ibuprofen as needed. Expect cramping and period-like discharge.

My clothes go back on in the order I took them off: Bra. Sweatpants. Sweatshirt.

Rebecca pushes open the back door to reveal the sun up and shining, a bright and open parking lot, loaded with more protestors, more shouting, and with the jacket over me again, I rush into the light.

PART THREE:

The Difficult Kind

CHAPTER 22

I pull into the parking lot of Stellar's Jay. A painting of its namesake, a blue and black bird with white markings on its face, is on the window. I've been here once, sometime last year. A poetry reading with Daniel. We sat for three uncomfortable hours in wooden chairs while about twenty people read long poems about how some things are scary and other things aren't and in life, there is fluidity and rabbits and between their poems, they told stories about how they wrote the poems with fountain pens, and I was like, Daniel, you're killing me, and he was like, don't listen, feel.

When I walk into Stellar's Jay today, who do I see? A naked Adrienne with a gun in her mouth. A series of self-portraits line the walls. Adrienne, the live version herself, is nearby in black pleather platform boots laced up to her thighs, a long black skirt, and a black bustier tied in the back with red ribbon. She passes flyers to people. The name of her show, NEMATODE, in bold, red letters. The back of her card says she's a photographer for hire.

"Is that a real gun?" I ask.

"Yes," she says and moves away.

Though I seem to have finished most of the bleeding, I still have a light level of discharge and vague cramping. I question myself, only now, if I should have brought an extra pad. I push out a piece of Nicorette gum in a blister pack. An older woman next to me clicks her tongue.

"You're trying to quit?" she asks.

She is as tall as the tallest man in this room and wears dark green thick glasses. Her hair is curly and dyed red. This is someone's mother? Whose?

"I am," I say.

"Do you know how I quit? None of that stuff. The gum. The patch. Forget it. You gotta cut the line," she says. "Cut it off."

185

"Oh?"

"I rented a cabin in the woods," she says. "I locked myself inside for three days. Every time I wanted a cigarette, I ate a banana."

"That worked?"

"Been two years. Haven't had a cigarette since," she says. "Don't want one. Don't need one."

She reaches into her purse, passes me a card. Elizabeth Montgomery, L.P.C.

"I help people quit," she says and walks off.

Card tables set up near the front door hold sugar cookies, boxes of wine, and cans of PBR. I pour myself a large cup of the wine. This place smells musty. A girl bumps into the table and some cookies fall to the floor. She picks them up and tries not to look at anyone. The scene in here is a fire hazard. Lots of people crammed into a small space filled with old wood.

Most people who mill in immediately walk through Adrienne's photographs. Suddenly, in the crowd, a young woman yells out, "rage!" We all stop, turn our attention to her, even Adrienne. With shaky hands, she produces a sheet of paper.

"He offered me a slice of orange/I pointed to my mouth/said I'd just brushed my teeth/so that would not work at all," the girl continues.

Jesus. Is this performance art?

"We are wolves!" she cries out. "We are splitting in two!"

Christ. What is happening?

There's a guy next to me who smells like pot. He looks bored, too. We catch each other's eye. He smiles a little. I smile a little back. Then the light changes. He turns colors, his face changes, becomes ghastly and strange.

The room looks hazy now. Some of the cigarette air has found its way in and hovers in the air, stuck, unattached. Craving. The smoke wafts into the room through the open window. I spit my dead gum into the trash and start to walk outside, ready to bum a cigarette from the first person I see but another card on the cookie table catches my eye.

Emotional Garage Sale.

Do you have items of emotional significance you are willing to sell or trade? Aurora Dahl welcomes your items the second Saturday of every month. All contributions big or small welcome. It's time to take stock and start clean.

She's making the rounds. The back of the card—it's more like a postcard, actually—shows her address. I fold it and put it in my pocket. The bracelet catching on my jeans.

"Shannon," a voice says from behind me. I turn. It's Daniel.

He's in all black. He's cut his hair. It's styled, nice, and somehow changes the structure of his face, which has a little bit of beard growth. Just enough. He's different, and it's not only the way he looks.

"Oh my god. You cut your hair?"

"I did. It was time for a change."

"I've called," I say.

"Yeah, I know," he says. "Been busy. The patio is being fixed. The owners came out, they were pissed."

"It was an accident," I say.

He shrugs. "Maybe. Still caused a lot of damage. They've asked us to leave."

"Oh my god."

"We have until the end of the month," he says.

"Daniel. I'm so sorry."

"Yeah, thanks," he says, almost surprised. "I appreciate that."

"I am sorry," I say again. "I'm sorry."

He flinches at this, and I know that he knows about Adrian. And I know that he knows that I know he knows. We stare at each other. My Daniel. My best friend. The only person who has offered unconditional love for me.

"Listen—"

"I have a few things to do before we start," he says and walks off.

I feel desperate. "Can I help you? I can help."

"You should find a seat," he says over his shoulder. "It's filling up."

"OK. Right. Good luck. Or, break a leg. I don't know what I'm supposed to say."

I eat a cookie, then I slip out. Ask a guy wearing a Beatles t-shirt for a smoke. He offers me a shitty Parliament. I ask him for a light, which he tries to do for me, but I take the lighter out of his hand then hand it back, walk away and smoke by myself. Not into the smoker's chitchat right now.

Through this window, I see more of Adrienne's photographs. Adrienne stands in the middle with her hands clasped in front of her. She's fully clothed in the first few. Not unlike what she's wearing tonight. Pleather. Strings. Corset. Ties. As we progress, she's more and more naked. Then the gun creeps in. First, she's looking at it. Then holding it. Then she's got in her mouth.

"Those photographs are so great," a girl says walking up next to me. She lights a cigarette. "So evocative."

I don't answer.

Unimpressed with me, she says, "It's about suicide."

"Right."

"What do you think of the title?"

"Nematode?" I ask. "Well, it totally fits."

"How so?" she responds in a way that now feels like a trick.

"Um, you know, it just does."

I watch Adrienne through the window greet two other people: one in a pair of bright red pants, and another in a baby doll dress and tights and Vans. The three of them hug. They kiss the air around each other.

I'm feeling boozy but not drunk; I'm still me. Wine doesn't do enough to take everything away. Wine makes the edges blurry. That's all.

I'm about to extinguish my cigarette when Adrian walks up.

"Adrian!"

He turns, sees me. Smiles. Does not offer anything else.

From inside Stellar's Jay, music starts. "I gotta go," he says.

A girl and guy holding hands walk through the gallery and gape at Adrienne's photographs. The girl looks from the gun photo to Adrienne herself and says, "Wow."

Adrienne blushes.

The girl says, "Beautiful."

"Thank you," Adrienne says.

I should probably have some water, instead, I go in and pluck a can of beer out of the cooler before I sit down in one of the folding chairs that's been put out. My beer can is dripping wet. My hand is wet. The can sweats. I shake my hand to get the extra water off, and the water splatters on the old wood floor.

The door opens behind me, and I look over my shoulder to see Rebecca, also dressed in all black. I wave. I pat the seat next to me. She waves back, but she bypasses me and approaches Daniel and Adrian, who have made an appearance near the front of the room by the fireplace. Daniel pulls a sheet off an object and reveals a puppet stage. Rebecca's back is to me, so when Daniel hugs her, I see him reach for her ass and squeeze it. Adrienne pats me on the shoulder. "This is going to be a great show," she says and takes a seat two rows up from me.

"Folks," Daniel says and the dull murmurs quiet down. He looks confident and welcoming. "Good evening and thank you for coming out. Steller's Jay, I'm so very honored to be able to present my friends here tonight. We have a very fine story for you. A very fine story indeed. We have betrayal. We have the rape of the human heart. But mostly, we have love. We have a hell of a story about love. I'd like to thank everyone who was a part of this production for putting up with all my creative angst—especially at the end here when I pretty much rewrote the entire back end of this thing. I'd like to introduce our esteemed puppeteers. Mr. Adrian Harandi and Mr. Gabriel Juarez. Sirs, please, take your applause."

Adrian and this guy Gabriel, who I have never seen in my life, bows and everyone claps. It's like he fell out of the air.

"Lastly, please, everyone, honor this lovely young lady who, tonight for the first time, is lending her magnificent vocal stylings to our humble marionette production, Ms. Rebecca Mason."

The fuck? Rebecca puts her hands to her cheeks while everyone claps for her. She then steps up and puts her arm around Daniel's shoulder. "And Mr. Daniel Parrish, everyone. Benton's own Hemingway."

I mean. Hemingway? That's a stretch but—

Daniel bows his head, clearly overwhelmed at the attention. He's glowing. Brighter than the sun itself.

The lights dim and a spotlight highlights the stage. We're all dark now. Corbin, who is handled by Adrian, and Violet, who is handled by Gabe, appear on the stage for a few moments. Violet courtesies, and Corbin tips his hat. The crowd hushes and waits for what's next. The room is eerie now, still, like a shoreline without birds.

CHAPTER 23

Fast, old-timey piano music plays overhead. Is someone playing a piano? Or? I think about my grandparents. Music they'd like. The marionettes, Corbin and Violet, march out with knees high onto the stage in time with the beat. Corbin walks first, Violet immediately behind. I remember when Adrian first started messing around with puppets. His original movements were jerky and string-focused. As I watch Corbin move now, I think about how far he's come. His body is fluid; his steps are real. Violet, too. Adrian worked out all his kinks on Corbin, and Violet has always come off very well. She's looking out at all of us and doesn't realize he stops. She bumps into him.

"Why I oughta," Violet says, putting her fists up.

It's Rebecca. She's voicing Violet. She sits with Daniel, holds a little flashlight over the script. Rebecca makes Violet into a high-pitched, borderline hysterical 1930s heroine. Her voice is not bad, not at all.

"You oughta what?" Corbin straightens.

Daniel voices Corbin, which throws me a bit. Corbin always sounds like Adrian, just regular old Adrian and his regular old voice, but now he's Daniel, but not just Daniel. Daniel and someone else. He sounds like an old movie. Like Cary Grant. His speech is deliberate, enunciated, deeper, maybe a beat or two below the sound of his normal voice. A foreign voice. A stranger's voice.

"Oh, it's just you."

"It's *just* me." Corbin thumbs in her direction and shakes his head. "This one over here. No respect." Then he points to himself.

Violet makes a quarter turn away from him and cocks her hip.

"No respect. Ha! What about me? Where's my respect? Why do you always get to come out first?"

"I'm the lead. The leader. I have to come out first. I have to show you how it's done."

He kicks a leg up then, Michael Jackson-esque, and stops to wait for her reaction.

"I can do that, too." Violet struts for a moment, then poses. "I can do it better, even." She shimmies and then jumps, then poses, then kicks.

Violet takes a big breath and starts to sing. "Anything you can do I can better, I can do anything better than you."

"No, you can't," Corbin sings back, then jumps, twice.

But Daniel can't really sing, and I snicker a bit. No one else snickers. I cover my mouth and pretend like I had to cough.

"Yes, I can." Violet jumps three times.

"No, you can't." Corbin kicks his right leg twice.

"Yes, I can, yes, I can!" Violet kicks her right leg three times and her left leg once.

"No," Corbin kicks his leg four times, but then stops and stumbles. "Wait, maybe you can." He holds his leg up, which dangles from the joint at the knee. "Vi?"

"Yes, Cor," she says, dripping with sweet.

"It hurts when I do this." He kicks his leg up again.

"Cor?"

"Yes, Vi?"

"Then don't do that."

The audience laughs. The music begins again, and Violet moves toward Corbin, but then stops. She shrinks a bit, her head hangs low and her arms go floppy to her sides.

"Now what? What's wrong with you?" Corbin asks. "Are you injured better than me, too?"

"Ugh. I just, I don't know." Violet lifts her head and starts moving her arms all around her to emphasize how big she thinks her problem is.

"Oh *boy*," Corbin says.

"It's nothing, really," she says.

"Oh *geez*."

Violet walks to the edge of the stage and speaks over the audience's head. "I'm just in this—like, this thing. There's just this non-specific strangeness, this sort of vague, blah thing going on here." She moves her hands around her mid-section. "I feel, very, kind of, you know, icky, around inside."

"Come on, now, Vi. You don't need that. You're better than that. Just shake it off." Corbin approaches her and shakes his whole body, "Yeah, like this."

"That's not helping," she says.

A few people behind me laugh.

Corbin puts his hand up to his chin, like he's thinking. Then he gives an excited jump. "Say, I have an idea. Let me get you something."

She crosses her arms and pouts. "There's nothing you could get me, save for a complete new life, that would make me feel better."

"How about a piece of pie? You like pie. I'll get you some pie."

"Do you want me to get fat?"

"Oh Lord in Heaven, save me. Pie is good for you. It's sugar. Sugar makes you happy."

"Nothing makes me happy. I am the most unhappy person in the world. I refuse to be anything other than unhappy."

Corbin thinks about it. "Say, how about I sing you a song? You like songs. Songs make you happy."

"Cor. You can't really sing. Everybody knows it."

"I have a plan for that."

Corbin lifts his hand in the air as though to snap. "Maestro?"

I can't see who's playing, but I hear a live guitar. The first few notes pay homage to that opening piano jam, but then it slows down, modernizes. It turns into an indie-rocker-acoustic guy looking for his soul in the middle of an empty bar. Then Rebecca begins to sing. Corbin moves around like he's singing, and Violet doesn't do anything, just kind of listens. But they've clearly switched roles.

> *I never really knew what love could do/ Until the day I laid my eyes on you*
> *'cause love is somethin' I could never see, it has been mystery!*

"Gee, Corbin, you have an awfully high singing voice," Daniel says, trying to imitate Rebecca as Violet.

The audience laughs and claps. I don't laugh, but I do clap, just because everyone else is doing it. Then I put my hands back in my lap. The beer mixes with some of that dark black inside me, and the one, two clap is all I can pull out of myself because Rebecca's voice coming out of Corbin, coming out of Daniel, is doing something crazy to me. It's jealousy. I know that. But it's also sadness. I feel like I'm running a race and everyone's finished. I'm struggling for breath here, and everyone is celebrating their finish.

> *Gee, but I'd like to make you happy*
> *Oh honey!*

Rebecca starts singing the way women used to sing, all tinny and warbly. But as the song progresses, she makes it into her own and projects herself out to the audience. Like, her karaoke is a tropical storm, but her true voice is a category five hurricane.

> *I like to do*
> *What you like to do*
> *Our love will be so strong*

Violet, who just stands there and does nothing, takes Corbin's hand—rather, they touch fingertips because string puppets can't really hold hands—and together they step back

and forth across the stage in synchronicity. Corbin jumps, and
Violet jumps. They follow each other, and they stay in step
with each other, and they help each other out. They clearly can
anticipate the other's moves. Rebecca continues to sing for
them. They tap their toes and move their hips in exact rhythm
with each other.

When Corbin/Rebecca finishes singing, then
Violet/Daniel clears her throat. Rebecca begins speaking for
Violet again, and Daniel resumes speaking for Corbin and they
return to their roles. People in the audience clap like crazy.
They cheer. A guy whistles and claps. All of that right now?
It's going right into Rebecca's head. I turn to the guy who
whistled. Seriously. It will all go into her head.

Corbin looks expectantly at Violet who nods and then
says, "Yeah, maybe, but…"

"But what? What *now*?" Corbin stomps his foot. "What
else could you possibly want?"

"But you're singing that song because we're just
friends, right?" Violet asks. "I mean, I can't really do a love
thing right now."

The audience goes, "Awwww."

A man whistles again. Then says, "Hey, girl."

Violet perks up. "Hello? Hello out there?"

Violet attempts to fix her hair and smooth out her
dress. "Corbin? How do I look? A strange man is calling me
and I'm going to go to him in what will ultimately result in
another painful mistake. But I'll see you again soon when it
doesn't work out. I'll expect you to be waiting by the phone."

I don't look at Corbin anymore. I look at Daniel's face
in the flashlight reading his lines. I watch his lips move, giving
voice to Corbin, who talks to Violet, who begs Violet to
understand something.

You're my best girl.
Stay with me.
I love you.

I swing my gaze back over to Corbin, whose body is full of sadness, and Violet, whose head tilts toward the man's voice. I will him to look up at me, but if he feels me he doesn't acknowledge it and continues with his lines.

Corbin calls out to Violet, "We could have been something together, don't you think? We could have been so beautiful."

It seems like Violet is taking this in but then she shakes her head and kind of collapses. "Nah, I gotta go smear myself along every guy I see in front of you to make you feel bad on purpose. See you later, sucker!" Violet skips off.

Corbin hangs his head. The audience cries out in protest. They are ready to riot for Corbin. They really are. The mob turns against Violet in a flash.

Boo, Violet.

Booooo. Whore!

Corbin begins a slow tap dance without music. Daniel clucks his tongue for the sound effect. I try to stand. The audience begins to clap for him, and as the audience claps, he dances more and the music picks up, and the audience continues to clap until they are roaring for Corbin, and Corbin sucks in all that energy and kicks his legs higher and higher until he stops when the music stops. Corbin takes a bow. Violet does not return. Adrian, Daniel, Gabriel, and Rebecca all walk in front of the stage, hold hands up in the air and bow as a collective. The crowd seizes them.

CHAPTER 24

The soupiness of the performance room oozes out as people finally emerge from the gallery. I step outside on the porch to smoke. Rebecca spills out in a group of people, gushing and alive.

"Did you see me? I was fucking awesome. Man, I am on fucking fire," she says. She takes a long swing from her can of beer. "That was so awesome. So fucking awesome."

A guy in big pants taps her on the shoulder. "That was a really great performance," he says.

"Thank you," she says and puts her hands on her heart. "Thank you so much."

"You have a beautiful voice," Pants says.

"How long have you been planning this?" I ask her.

"What?" She shrugs. "I don't know. A while." She waves to someone who is waving to her. She rolls her eyes then. "What, are you upset? It's entertainment."

"How long have you been sneaking off to hang out with Daniel?"

She smiles. "I told you he and I slept together."

"Um…yeah, I thought it was one night?"

"Jealous? Finally?"

"No."

"Daniel is, I don't know. He's one of the good ones," she says. "He asked me to be a part of his art. He thinks I am also an artist with my voice. I had to say yes."

This Pants guy lingers. He's Rebecca's type. Older. Flattering the shit out of her.

"So you and Daniel are friends with benefits?" I am incredulous.

"Yes. Or no. Maybe something more. I don't know. There's a connection. He's also just really good at it. You know, at sex." This guy near her pretends to look around at other things, but he's listening. "Makes me feel special. Like, he's in it for me. I've never, ever had that. He literally exists in that bedroom for my pleasure." She laughs at herself. "He is ribbed for my pleasure."

"Daniel is not the using for sex type of guy."

She laughs. "Every guy is a use for sex kind of guy."

The Pants guy is close still, so I turn to him. "Can I help you?"

"I was waiting to talk to her," he says, points to Rebecca who puts her hand under her chin as if to say *"who me?"*

"He's sensitive," I say and pull her arm away from both Pants and the door where more people come out, any of whom might be Daniel. "He'll get feelings, and he will be weird with you about them."

She looks dreamy for a minute.

"I bet he wouldn't cheat on me," she says.

I try to change course.

"Why are you so into Daniel all of a sudden?"

"Hey," she says, "I was in pain, and he has been fucking it out of me. And it's working."

We're interrupted by the door swinging open and Adrian and Adrienne blow past us. Adrienne ahead, all her photographs tucked under her arm. She marches into the street and holds them over her head.

"What's going on?" I ask.

Rebecca shrugs.

Adrienne tosses one of the photographs on the street, the first one, the one where's fully dressed. "This is how you look to other people," she shouts.

People gather around her. She tosses another. The one where she's taken off her jacket and shirt, and she's in her bra. "This is a father who doesn't protect you," she shouts.

She tosses another. "This is a mother who doesn't believe you."

Another. "This is a teacher who uses you because he can."

Another. She's fully nude. "This is how you destroy yourself."

The gun in her mouth. "This is how you save yourself."

She holds a rolled-up newspaper in the air and lights it with a set of matches. I step off the porch and walk toward her through the crowd of people.

"NEMATODE!" she screams and throws the newspaper onto her photographs.

Holy shit. I jump back.

A slow flame crawls along her face, the paper curls in on itself, then spread out in a flash. She wasn't careful when she threw them, so they're splayed out far and wide. Adrienne looks wild and hot. Unbothered. Strong. She's breathing hard like she's been fighting.

"Shannon," I hear a voice yell out. Rebecca. "Fillies is doing bar karaoke. Are you coming?"

Daniel sidles up next to her and takes her hand, stares me down. She nudges him and they start walking. I follow behind, alone.

In the distance, I hear sirens. Someone called the fire department. Adrienne's pictures are all ablaze now. She has a bottle of water and throws some of it on one part of the fire but doesn't get it all out.

"Hey," she yells out as more people back away. "Hey! Help!"

A man runs out with a hose and starts spraying everything down. I run to catch up with Rebecca and Daniel. They're ahead of me, hands clasped, heads bent toward each other. At one point, the silhouette of Rebecca tosses her head back and laughs.

The train tracks are ahead of us. We'll have to cross them to get to Fillies. The lights are flashing, and the bell is dinging. The sidewalk is coated with old gum and cigarette butts and wrappers and cups and cans. People are fucking out of control with their littering. Daniel pulls Rebecca under the arms, and she screams but in a happy way, and the two of them jet across the tracks before the light of the train is upon us. I am stuck behind the roar, the red lights beating my skin, and I notice there's green glass all around me. Heineken bottles, I guess. An expensive bottle to break.

CHAPTER 25

The sounds of the Fillies karaoke crowd blast me even from the sidewalk. First Friday makes the downtown extra insane. Rebecca pushes through the bar and beelines for the karaoke leader. A group of people stand up, appearing to leave, so I throw myself on the table as a server approaches and clears off their garbage. Daniel sits down and asks the server for two shots and two beers. I assume these are not for me. He will not look at me or acknowledge me, but I stand there awkwardly anyway. Daniel freezing me out feels awful. I'm about to reach for him, say—something, anything—when two things happen. Rebecca throws down the big karaoke book and opens it, and there's a tap on my shoulder.

The opening riff to a Madonna song begins. The person singing, a man, is bad.

When I turn, I see the hotshot's face. He is in the same clothes he was in when I met him. White button-down shirt and jeans. He's smiling at me. Funny us bumping into each other in this place again.

"Buy you a drink?" he asks.

The server is back to their table with Daniel and Rebecca's drinks, so I duck away from them, follow the hotshot, turning back only once to see Rebecca on Daniel's lap, his arms around her waist, his mouth in her neck. We make eye contact for a brief second, and that is all it takes for me to understand what I think he's doing. Rebecca leans down and kisses him. Long, passionate, deep, and I do not give him the satisfaction of staring anymore.

"What do you want?" the hotshot yells over the music.

"Screwdriver!" I yell back.

He waves over a server. He leans forward, takes his Zippo out of his pocket and lights a cigarette then offers one to me. I accept. He flicks the Zippo but makes me lean toward him, and I do it.

When my drink arrives, I swallow half of it in one gulp. The wine and beer from earlier gone, the edges hard again. I keep my back to Daniel.

"How have you been?" the hotshot asks.

My ass is numb from the hard seat. I shift a little to change weight, and, like, a little bubble, the last of the assault, comes out of me and settles into the pad.

"Fine, and you?" I ask.

"Good. You want another one?" he asks.

My glass is ice. Sure, I'll take another. He plays with the Zippo. Snapping it open and closed. Metal on metal unpleasant.

"That's a nice lighter," I say.

"Yeah, it's my favorite," he says. "It was my dad's." He sets it on the table again.

"What are you up to after this?" he asks.

"I don't know," I say as I see Adrian wandering through the crowd, alone, looking for, I suspect, Daniel. I don't draw his attention.

The karaoke host stands off to the side holding up a slip of paper and mouthing whatever words are on it. She's tall with a long, deeply lined face, like a bitter man made her with a carving knife. Her platinum blonde hair (clearly, a wig) is under a black cowboy hat. She's dressed in a puffy white shirt with pink fringe hanging off the arms, skintight dark jeans, a turquoise belt buckle the size of a small child's head and pink cowboy boots. I recognize her. She's hosted in the past. During lulls in the karaoke, she fills the void with June Carter tunes.

Rebecca's up. She goes the torch song route. Dusty Springfield. She thought she had real feelings for Gary. Now she's singing to Daniel. She's singing right to him. I gulp my second drink down and feel the familiar pull of the blur, everything inside me smearing, running.

Rebecca touches Daniel's hair. He smiles up at her.

Maybe he senses me staring because he stares into me as the hotshot leans toward me and nuzzles my neck. Then,

Daniel gives me the most terrible look. The harshest, most horrifying look that for a second I think he must see someone he hates behind me. I move away from the hotshot and look, but there's no one, nothing, just me.

Adrian sits down next to Daniel then. Adrienne nowhere in sight. I imagine she's getting arrested for arson. Rebecca finishes her song to uproarious applause. Daniel stands for her. I sit here at this table with the hotshot and now two of his bros who have been, for some reason, wrestling with each other so hard they bump into the hotshot then bump into me. The Zippo, which he'd left out on the table standing up falls over in surrender. As the hotshot turns to his wrestling friends—who are, really, getting pretty into it with each other like in a way that feels scary but also makes me wonder how they really feel about each other—I reach for the Zippo and take it. Slip it into my pocket. Stand and walk away, go to Rebecca and nod for her to follow me. She frowns, not now. She's looking for another song. I take her arm.

"I have to go to the bathroom and so do you," I say.

"No, I really don't."

"You totally do, come on."

As we walk and pass many eligible men I say, "Anyone but Daniel."

There's a line to the bathroom, so much so that we're still out in the bar, leaning against the wall.

"What? Now you're saying that?"

"Yeah. Now I'm saying it."

"I think, honestly, Shannon, that ship sailed. I think it's too late."

"I don't want to fuck Daniel." I say but I am suddenly not sure if I believe it anymore. What if Rebecca was right? "But I think it's not a good idea for you to get involved with him now. I think he's—"

How do I say it? I think he's mad at me. I know he's mad at me. He's being a dick. My best friend Daniel is being a shitty asshole and as much as Rebecca is aggravating, I don't want her to get hurt either.

"I think Daniel is a mess right now for a bunch of reasons," I say.

We're in line for the bathroom. I feel drunk but not plastered. I'm less drunk than I usually am—a strange feeling. The inside of Fillies really is kind of a hole but it doesn't usually matter. In my mind's eye, I see the way Daniel stared at me while Rebecca was dancing over him. Something cracked in me when I saw his face.

"Daniel knows about you and Adrian," she says.

Hearing this out loud should not shock or upset me because I already knew. And yet a deep, icy pit forms in my stomach.

"It hurt his feelings," she says. "So, see? He's already hurt. We're mutually hurt people fucking each other. Relationships are built on less."

"So now it's a relationship?"

"God, I don't know what it is. No labels. You are more concerned about this than I am or he is."

We move forward again so now we're in the actual bathroom, which is, small, cramped, with only two stalls, one of them out of order and a vague sewer and beer smell that seems to be coming out of the walls and coating our skin.

I can't respond to this so I cross my arms.

"I didn't do it to hurt him."

"Why did you?"

"Why did I fuck Adrian? I don't know. I don't know. It just happened."

The stall opens and out walks Adrienne. Rebecca freezes. Adrienne heard us. I know she did. But instead, she checks herself in the mirror, fusses with her hair then flounces out of the bathroom.

"Oh shit," Rebecca says. "She heard. Do you think she heard? She heard. Oh shit, oh shit."

I rush out of the bathroom behind Adrienne and go to the table. I'm too late. She's pulled Adrian up by the arm and she's talking to him, gesturing to the bathroom. She raises her hand, then she hits him in the arm. Daniel stands, tries to step between them. Takes Adrienne's arm and attempts to move her. They all look at me when I approach. Daniel, like someone has killed his dog in front of him. Adrian, bewildered and beleaguered, but that's what he always looks like, and Adrienne, burning with rage. She points a long finger at me. "You fucking whore." She stomps out, Adrienne follows.

The brutality of her words upends me. I cross my arms, hang my head, and no one comes to comfort me. Not Daniel. Not Rebecca.

I do not know what to do.

The karaoke leader comes back on the mic. She says the next person up is Daniel Parrish and Rebecca Mason for a duet. The two of them take hands, walk to the mic together. I glance over at the hotshot who is on his hands and knees under the table looking for what he lost. I slip a cigarette out of the pack on the table—I don't know who it belongs to—and go outside, put the cigarette between my lips and use his Zippo to light it. Adrienne is screaming at Adrian, but she doesn't see me.

Vaguely, from inside Fillies, a tone deaf Daniel warbles *Hey Jude*.

Adrian is crying actual tears and then he drops onto his knees and buries his head in his hands. "I fucked up. I was fucked up. I didn't know what I was doing."

Adrienne hovers over him.

"I was really fucked up," Adrian repeats. "Really fucked up. But I'm going to get better, ok? Ok? I'll get better. I love you."

I start to walk away. Back toward my car, toward Stellar's Jay. Please, please, please don't leave me—Adrian's voice, pleading. I don't hear anything else. I don't know what she says to him.

I'm not sober, but I can drive. I drive myself home. Go into my room and lock the door. I put the second *White Album* disc into my CD and try to do as Daniel instructed, let it heal me. I wake up during *Why Don't We Do It In the Road?* when I hear Daniel and Rebecca come into the apartment, singing the Beatles and sounding like they can't live without each other.

CHAPTER 26

The sun is warm on my face. I lift my chin, close my eyes and feel its heat. I put the cigarette out in the empty ashtray. The butt is all alone in there, all curled up and used. I'm a little hungover but not like usual. I go back inside and start a pot of coffee. Tomorrow, I'm supposed to show up for my new job on campus. I would have called Daniel about it or dropped in on him at Hadley's, but that option is long gone. Rebecca comes out of her room in a robe then stops and closes her door all the way shut.

Rebecca opens the dishwasher and pulls out the Hadley's mug. She puts one foot on the other and perches like a flamingo. She smiles at me. The coffee finishes.

I grit my teeth. She holds out her mug. I pour for her. "How was the rest of your night?" I ask but I don't care.

"Amazing," she says and rolls her eyes up. "How was yours?" She removes a second mug from the dishwasher, pours coffee into it.

She opens the fridge and dumps half & half into each one. Daniel doesn't like his coffee that way, I almost say, but who cares. I pour my own coffee, turn the TV on, flip channels.

"Wait, wait, stop," Rebecca says and walks up to the TV. She points. "Isn't that your hotshot boyfriend?"

"Ashlee Ross is with our local hotshot team right now," says the anchor. "Ashlee? What do you have for us this morning?"

The reporter, Ashlee Ross, wears a red polo shirt and her hair back in a ponytail. The camera pans behind her, and a crew, fully decked out, carries a hose somewhere off screen.

"Captain," Ashlee Ross says as a large man fills the screen, "tell us what, exactly, what you're planning to do and what this dry season has in store for us."

"The good news, Ashlee, is it looks like we've got some rain coming up, and this dry winter we've had should give way to a wet spring. But beyond that, controlled burns are a healthy part of forest management."

The camera pans behind them again. I look close to the screen. I see him. He's right there. He's in full gear, with his helmet held off to the side. He approaches the camera and smiles at Ashlee Ross.

"What's your name?" she asks.

"Kevin," he says.

"Kevin, how long have you been with this hotshot crew?" she asks.

He's out of breath. "This is my second season. Maybe if you want me to be technical, one and a half. My first full fire season. I joined up last year."

"And why do you do what you do? What do you get out of it?"

He smiles at her. "It's not really about me, it's about doing a public service, it's about being a part of my community, protecting my community."

Ashlee Ross giggles. "We're all grateful for your service. All of you heroes going out into that danger."

He laughs. "No, not me. I'm not a hero."

She beams into the camera. "But they are heroes, Rob. These hotshot crews are out here risking their lives for us. And that is a *hot* topic indeed. Back to you in the studio."

I roll my eyes. Turn off the TV as Daniel comes into the living room. He's dressed. All black, his clothes from last night.

"Oh Shannon," Rebecca says coming up to me. She picks up my wrist. "I never noticed this. Your bracelet. It's so cute."

I touch the little e. "Thank you," I say, pointedly.

She turns to Daniel and hands him a mug of coffee.

"I'm going to take a shower," she says. "Trust me, I need one."

He sips it, all the while staring at me then sinks into the couch next to me. Daniel and I have certainly spent nights together but separately. I've seen him in the mornings. This isn't new. What is new is the look in his eyes. He's feral. His eyes are wild. For the first time in our history, I can't read him. Or, God, could I ever? He feels like he's challenging me, which is confusing. It's not a sporty challenge either. His energy feels angry.

We're not friends anymore. Because friends don't look at each other like this.

"Hi," he says.

"Hi," I respond.

"Had fun last night?" I ask.

"I did."

"Great."

"And you."

"Oh, I always have fun."

"Of course."

"Hadley's is all done?" I ask.

"Pretty much."

"You and Rebecca hanging out today?"

"I have to go back to my house. Adrian leaves later on."

"Where's he going?"

"Adrienne's uncle has a place in Montana. They're going to dry out."

"Huh."

"Yeah."

"Adrienne doesn't seem like the Montana type."

"People are surprising."

"I don't think so. I think people are not really that surprising."

"Adrian needs open spaces. He needs to get away from the bad things."

He says bad things in a way that makes me feel like I'm the bad things though I don't know if it's me or him making me feel this way.

The water turns on. Rebecca is in the shower. I half except him to go join her, but he stays put.

I think about the first time I met Adrian. Daniel had a party at his old place. Adrian showed up, high as shit but in good spirits. He was funny, lively. The next morning, we all woke up together, half on the couch on the floor, and I went out for coffee for everyone. Adrian sat at the kitchen table as Daniel told him highlights of the party, how Adrian played his guitar, stood on the table and sang "The Devil Went Down to Georgia" and also the entire Oasis catalogue. We all contain multitudes. The Adrian I left outside Filles last night is not the same Adrian. But maybe neither am I. Neither is Daniel.

Daniel leans over and looks into my mug, which is almost empty. He stands, gets the coffee pot and pours more coffee for me.

"Adrienne isn't a monster," Daniel says.

"Did I say she was?"

"Yes."

I mean, I thought we were in agreement about her sucking but maybe not.

"You doing ok?" Daniel asks. This is the old Daniel. The question between us feels painful, like bumping a bruise. As soon as he asks, it feels like he wants to take it back. He forgot himself. He forgot his own agenda here.

"Getting through it all," I say. I tuck my leg under me.

"Job?"

"New one starting soon."

"What happened to the old one?"

"Fired."

"Fired?"

"Yep."

"Huh. Why?"

"I kind of didn't go in for awhile," I say.

"That'll do it."

"I'm going to work for one of my professors. She's cool. I don't know. Maybe it'll be good. Every new beginning comes from some other beginning's end."

Daniel smirks. He wants to laugh but is afraid that will betray something. A real sense of loneliness has come over me, and whose fault it is, I am not sure.

"Do you remember—" I start to say but stop.

He leans forward, like he's ready to go down whatever road I'm willing to go down with him but I can't. It's all gone, and I can't.

"What?"

"Nevermind."

"Tell me."

"Why?"

"I want to know."

"You don't."

"Hey, there's a hot guy calling out for me outside. I better go get him," I say and sip my coffee. "I better abandon myself and my friends for some validation."

Daniel raises his eyebrow at me.

Rebecca opens her door. "I'll be ready in like 10 minutes." She closes it again.

"It'll be 25," I say.

"You didn't say thank you," Daniel says.

"What?"

"I poured more coffee for you. You didn't say thank you."

I laugh, but he's serious.

"Daniel," I say and put my hand on his knee. "*Thank you.*"

He snorts a little but it's because he thinks I'm being ridiculous. I pull my hand back. Stand up. "I have shit to do today," I say.

When I rinse my mug, I notice a stack of mail on the counter. Rebecca must have grabbed it. Bills. Bills. Overdue.

Fuck me. Then a card. My mother's handwriting. I rip it open and about eight twenties fall to the floor. Daniel stands over me as I pick them up.

"What's that for?"

I read the card. "I love you, Love MOM."

I stay on the ground, read the card over and over. I guess I'm on the ground so long Daniel bends down next to me. "Are you ok?"

His tone ignites something, and I jerk away. He puts his hands up. "Geez. Just trying to be nice."

I stand up, and he stands with me. We face off. But I don't want to deal with this, so I turn. He takes my arm. We both look down and he lets go. He grabbed me kind of hard.

"Wait," he says.

"I have to go," I say.

"Please, wait. I'm leaving. I bought a ticket to Paris. I'm leaving in a few days."

"With Rebecca?" I frown, legitimately cannot process what he's saying right now.

I hear her singing in the other room.

"No," he says. "By myself."

"That's what you wanted," I almost whisper. "To go to Paris to be Ernest Hemingway."

"No. I mean, yes. To write. Not to be Ernest Hemingway."

"You're going to break up with her?" I ask.

"We're not together," he says. "but listen. Listen. You could come with me. What if you came with me?"

"Are you crazy?"

"No. Let's do it. Shannon—I—"

We're so close I can smell the coffee in his breath. I can feel the heat of his body. In this moment, I take a complete inventory of every feeling I've ever had for him but nowhere in that do I find lust. Nowhere do I find the kind of love he wants. And now, after that show last night, something else, something confusing and strange. Distrust.

Rebecca comes out of her room, slips her arms around his waist and Daniel straightens up. Pleads with me but then that slowly turns to…what? To triumph?

"Hi lovey," she says and squeezes him.

Daniel is going to flatten her. Shatter her into a million pieces.

"Hi babe," he says and gives me a specific, direct look. And it feels like he's doing it on purpose to hurt me.

I go into my room, put some extra clothes on, grab my shoes and purse and get out the door. I take out my MapQuest directions and follow them until I get to the nice street in the nice neighborhood with the nice people. I open my trunk and pull out the box I'd packed up in there. My mother's clothing. The CDs Daniel has given me. The Hadley's mug I swiped from the sink and barely wiped it out. I slip off the bracelet. I hand over the Zippo.

She takes me into her garage. "This is your first time bringing things here?" she asks with Gracie the dog at her feet.

"Yes."

She unloads the box, picks through my mother's clothing They're the same age. Aurora oohs and aahs as she examines each skirt. Each pair of pants. Each sweater.

"All right, honey," she says. All my items on table in front of me.

A car goes by slowly, a stick crunches underneath the tires.

"I'll go get the form. You'll fill it out. Assign your prices," she says. "Back in a jiffy."

In the street, two walkers walk in tandem. An old man with his old dog strolls by on the opposite sidewalk. The sky is clear. All my inventory laid out on the table in front of me. Aurora is halfway to the door to the house.

"Wait," I say.

Acknowledgments

I wrote the first draft of this novel in 2006, and I have pulled it apart and put it back together, left it for dead and resurrected it more times than I can count. Shannon Story has been searching for home for almost 20 years, and I'm grateful to Adam Van Winkle and Cowboy Jamboree Press for finally giving her a place to rest. Thank you also to Dan Crawley, another Cowboy Jamboree author, who gave me the pep talk I needed in the moment I needed it.

Burn would not be here today without Liz Kay. I mean, literally. Liz suggested the title after countless other titles never felt right. She believed in this book from day one, and she never let me give up. (She let me scream and cry, but I wasn't allowed to give up.) Burn really is our book.

My endless thanks to my early readers who may read *Burn* today and not even recognize it but their willingness to indulge my bad first drafts meant a lot: Nicole Goodwin, Amy Vericker, Kate Tierney, and Kara Waite.

Deep gratitude to my UNMFA cohort: Natalia Treviño, Bill James, Jen Lambert, Ken Brosky, and especially Terry Kelly, who understood Shannon on a level I could not yet and spent hours and drinks and more drinks and more hours talking through her motivations with me. (Shout out to Mitch the Bartender at the Lied.) Additional thank you to my mentors during my time in that program: Richard Duggin, Jim Peterson, Amy Hassinger, and Catherine Texier.

It is always important to thank Tod Goldberg, and I do so here.

In one of its many eras, this novel existed as a linked story collection, and thus I offer my deep gratitude to the editors at *The Fiddlehead* and *JMWW Journal* for publishing "The Sink In Here Is Always Wet" in 2009, and "Monstrous and Curious Things" in 2022, respectively. I'm especially thankful to Danny Goodman who published "The Hotshot" in 2013 at *fwriction:*

review and Anna Zumbahlen and Matthew Limpede at *Carve Magazine* who published "The Difficult Kind" in 2017.

I am endlessly grateful to Josh Mohr and Decant Editorial, who taught me how to write a novel, and whose voice and editorial insight was and is invaluable.

Thank you to Michael Kiggins and his novel *And the Train Kept Moving*. Reading his book gave me the permission I needed to take Shannon's story back to the right time.

Thank you to my family, especially to my mother, who would move the sun if I asked her to. And to my sister, who is unlikely to read this book, and that is okay.

Finally, to my husband, stepson, and daughter (and our crazy dog, too): you are home to me.